Breathe Again

KIKO GARCIA

iUniverse, Inc.
New York Bloomington

Breathe Again

iUniverse books may be ordered through booksellers or by contacting:

iUniverse
1663 Liberty Drive
Bloomington, IN 47403
www.iuniverse.com
1-800-Authors (1-800-288-4677)

Because of the dynamic nature of the Internet, any Web addresses or links contained in this book may have changed since publication and may no longer be valid. The views expressed in this work are solely those of the author and do not necessarily reflect the views of the publisher, and the publisher hereby disclaims any responsibility for them.

ISBN: 978-1-4502-1387-5 (sc)
ISBN: 978-1-4502-1388-2 (ebook)
ISBN: 978-1-4502-1389-9 (dj)

Printed in the United States of America

iUniverse rev. date: 6/2/2010

Chapter One
the pool

It is a hot summer day in July. Fifteen-year-old Barbie Garcia is sitting by the Hialeah community pool waiting for her boyfriend, Eric. She has long brown hair and brown eyes that seem to sparkle when she laughs. Her body and charming manner make her look older than she is. Barbie's lifelong friend, Lisa, is with her, as usual.

"Hey, Barbie, is that a new bathing suit?"

"Yeah, Lisa, how do I look?"

"I think you are the second best looking girl here."

"Lisa, have you seen Eric and Javy?"

"Yeah, here comes Eric now!"

Eric has just finished changing into his swimming trunks. He is seventeen years old with a muscular build. He has black hair and hazel eyes. He is quiet and unassuming—a polite young man with a love of adventure, who is fearless to a fault.

"Hello, ladies. Nice suit, Barbie."

"Thanks Eric!" "By the way Eric where is your trusty sidekick Javy?"

"He's on his way you know Javy, never in any kind of a hurry."

As they speak, you can hear the distinctive sound of the diving board in the background, accompanied by a splash and the happy laughter of children romping in the water at the low end of the pool.

Suddenly, there is an anguished cry.

"Help me, please! Someone, please, help me! My brother needs help! Help him, please!" Running to the edge of the pool Barbie looks into the deep end of the pool.

"Oh, my God, Eric, look! There's someone at the bottom of the pool Barbie screams!"

Eric shades his eyes from the glare of the sun reflecting off the surface of the pool.

"Quick, Lisa, get the lifeguard! I passed her as she went into the ladies bathroom." Babie shots, as she looks back at Eric.

Without a moment's hesitation, Eric jumps in and heads for the bottom, where the boy lies motionless a few feet from the floor drain. The boy's eyes are still open, with no expression on his face.

Grabbing the boy by his arm, Eric pushes off from the bottom and begins pulling him toward the shallow end of the pool. Then he hears a loud splash behind him. Turning, he sees the lifeguard and Javy in the pool with him. Working together, they get the boy to the edge of the pool. The lifeguard takes over.

Lifeguard, "Keep his head as straight as you can! He may have spinal injuries! Alright now, on three let's lift him out of the water. One, two, three! Once out of the water she yells out. Anyone here know CPR?"

Eric replies, "Yes, I do. Okay, you begin compressions while I breathe for him."

As they work on the boy, Barbie kneels next to his limp body. With her hands clasped firmly together, she whispers over and over, "Breathe again. Breathe again."

The sound of the fire truck's siren is now so loud it sounds like the truck is going to drive over them. A few seconds later, the paramedics arrive.

All of a sudden the boy begins to cough up water and takes a deep, gasping breath. With this, the crowd lets out a loud cheer.

A grandmother who has witnessed the whole event comes running up, grabs Eric by both his hands and yells out, "I saw it! I saw it all! You are a hero!"

Eric begins to blush. "No, ma'am, I'm no hero."

The medics load the boy onto a stretcher and begin to wheel him toward their truck. Just then the boy's mom arrives.

"Is he going to be alright?"

"Yes ma'am, but he needs to go the hospital for observation."

"Thank you, sir! You saved my little boy's life." As she hold her sons hand.

"Ma'am, you need to thank this young man. He's the one who jumped in and pulled him out."

Giving him a hug. "Thank you for saving my son's life. How can I ever repay you? I have no money, but I will forever be grateful for what you did here today."

"You do not need to thank me ma'am, we all did it together."

"Yes, but you are the one that jumped in first and pulled him up, he could have drowned if not for you." The boys little sister tells them as she puts her arms around Eric's legs and gives him a hug.

Eric finds himself at a loss for words. As he turns to walk away, he bumps into the fire lieutenant standing behind him.

The fire lieutenant puts his hand on Eric's shoulder. "Good work, son, you saved his life!"

"Yeah, I guess I did, but I don't think it merits all this attention."

"Well, he's a hero and modest too! Have you ever thought about becoming a fireman, son?"

Javy chimes in, "Way to go, bud! You save a life and get a job all in one morning."

"Whoa, it's not quite that fast or easy, but we do hire every year, and it's a rewarding job. You should give it some thought."

"Thanks, I will!"

"No, son, thank *you*." The lieutenant tells him one more time as they pick up their gear and head back to the truck. He then turns to Pete.

"Hey, Pete, we might have a future rookie here!"

Pete retorts, "Yeah, if you want a job where you rush into a burning building where even the rats have sense enough to flee, you save the building, and the tenants complain that you used too much water or that you were too slow to get there—then this might be the job for you!"

Lieutenant, "Ah, don't mind Pete, he'd complain if they hung him with a new rope."

"See yah later, guys!"

"Yes, sir, good-bye."

As the crowd begins to dissipate Eric turns to Javy.

"Hey, Javy, have you ever thought about being a fireman?"

"No, I was thinking more of hunting and fishing for the rest of my life!"

"I'm serious, man. Have you ever given it any thought?"

"Maybe I would if they would let me carry a gun, too."

"Javy, you can't even carry a tune, much less a gun!"

"Very funny, Lisa!"

"Well, I think I'm going to give this more thought."

"You do that, mister hero. Alright, Lisa, let's challenge the hero and the future diva to a chicken fight."

"Okay, Javy, but this time you pick me up." Lisa chuckled.

Those care free days of summer are soon over and the pool incident is forgotten by all except Eric.

He now knows what he wants to be, with his mind made up to be a firefighter; he sets out to make his dream come true.

After graduation Eric goes on to college to get his fire science degree.

Javy enrolls in an air conditioning technical school, while Barbie focuses all her energy and talent into her singing.

One thing thy know will never change, the fact that the three will always be inseparable.

Chapter Two
At the fire station

EIGHT YEAR have passed since the day Eric saved the boys life. He took the fireman's advice after graduating from high school and   passed the fire department test; now after five years as a firefighter he was recently promoted to Lieutenant on C shift.

Station 3crews   consist of ten sometimes eleven firefighter , three on the ladder, three or four on the fire truck, three on the rescue and one chief for that zone his radio call numbers are 122.

When a someone is on vacation, sick or on RDO (regular day off, shift work consist of twenty four hours on and forty-eight off with an RDO every three weeks) personal of the same rank are sent to fill their spot. If the department is shorthanded someone that is qualified may fill in the spot. This is called ridding out of class.

Eric Montana is lieutenant, but he is ridding out of class as captain today, Mike Tanner is his driver, with Pete Jonson as third man on the ladder.

Bert Fernandez is lieutenant on recue 3 with paramedics Joe Garcia and Tommy Jones.

Eddy Jackson is lieutenant on fire truck 3 with and Andy Hernandez y driving and Howe Steel as third man.

Chief Allen Daniels is 122 for this station and all the north end of the city

A warm July Sunday morning finds them working C shift at station 3.

Eric, "Alright, listen up, girls! Today, I'm riding as acting captain. Eddy, you got Howe. Bert and his rescue prima donnas will be on

Rescue 3. And let's see … Pete will be acting alive for at least half the shift … That's it, ladies! Hey, Pete, we have a rookie on his way from station one. Show him what we do around here on Sundays!"

Bert, "For Peter, that would be watching TV, sleeping on the recliner, and complaining about the rescue and engine crew—especially complaining if he has to take a blood pressure on one of our fine upstanding citizens."

"Hey, Bert! When you were just a gleam in the trash man's eye, I was out here fighting fires and saving lives."

"And sleeping in the recliner, Pete?"

Just then the chief Daniels walks in "Carry on men."

"No! Well, maybe that one time!"

"Hey look, the rookie's here, and he looks real *GQ*, Pete!"

Pete looks at the rookie and grumbles, "Great! Another one of you pretty mama's boys!"

Mike laughs, "Pete, just because your mom had to tie a bone to your leg so the dog would play with you, doesn't mean we all had that problem!"

Pete, "Oh, yeah!"

Mike, "hey rookie you know how to use a mop?"

Yes sir.

Pete, "Did you hear that, he call Mike sir, hey rookie here we call Mike a lot of things, but sir is not one of them."

"Yes sir."

Mike, "Rookie do you know your radio signals yet?"

"Yes sir. QSL to let dispatch, or who ever calls know you got their message, QSK to proceed with a message also."

Mike, "That's enough, but can you cook?"

Just then, the loudspeaker blares out, "Rescue 3, Ladder 3, 122. We have a child pinned under a car at Milander Park!"

Chief, "One-two-two responding … have Hazmat 6 respond." "Ladder 3 and Rescue 3 responding." "Dispatch, QSL." Bert, "Rookie, get your gear and jump aboard rescue 3!"

Bert, "is Joe here?"

"Yes, I'm here!"

Bert, "Alright, ladies, let's ride."

They roar out of the station and into traffic.

Eric, who is watching for cars on his side, yells out. "Clear on the right, Mike, go, go, go! Come on, lady … big red truck coming through. Get the hell out of the way!"

Knowing Mike is focused on driving Eric shouts over the siren "Oh, my God, Mike, did you see that blonde in the red Honda?"

"No!" Mike replies with a big smile.

"You're clear on the right, Mike! Go, go, go!"

"Where was 122 responding from?"

"I don't know, Mike. City Hall is closed, so there's nobody to brown-nose today!"

"There they are Mike. Go ahead and drive on the grass. Get as close as you can to the car. Oh, boy, that does not look good!

The truck comes to a stop as close as they can get and a cloud of dust billows from under the vehicle as Mike sets the air brake. Two hundred feet in front of their ladder truck they can see a car with two small feet sticking out from underneath the front tires. A small crowd is already forming. Eric,"where the hells are the cops? We need crowd control!"

Eric, "Ladder 3 and Rescue 3 arrive."

Because of the severity of the accident additional manpower is needed. The haz/mat crew from station 6 will carry a three man crew and special equipment. The three man crew from station 5 will be used to set up a landing zone for the helicopter.

Dispatch, "ladder 3, will you need additional man power?"

Eric, "Dispatch, we will and, do you have more Hialeah PD units in route?"

Dispatch, "QSL Ladder 3, we have two more units responding."

Dispatch, "Engine 5 responds to Milander Park to assist ladder 3 with an LZ."

Engine5, "QSL, engine 5 responding!"

"Alright, Pete! Howe, you break out the jaws, yes sir Eric. Eric grabs the portable radio as he jumps out of the truck and calls rescue 3." Ladder 3 to Rescue 3." "QSK ladder 3."

"Bert, go to tact 2," QSL Ladder 3." "Bert go ahead and bring your rig on the other side of the mound."

"Got it Eric!"

"Eric yells out over the sound of approaching sirens, Pete, go ahead and start the jaws!"

Mike jumps in "Eric are you going to use the spreader on the jaws to lift one side of the car or the entire front end"?

Eric, "I think we can lift the entire front end Mike".

Eric "We need a more stable surface for the bottom plate to lift the whole front end!"

"Pete, get a two-by-six board and shove it under the spreader!"

"Mike, do you think a single two-by-six will hold all that weight Eric?"

Eric, "we don't have any other options; if we use more than one it will not give us enough room to get the spreader under the car. You men stabilize the front of the car! Pete, flip the switch and start her up. Joe, get ready to pull him out!"

Hazmat 6 arrives.

Bert," the hazmat truck here now Eric!" "I know Bert, but he is under the engine and he might be getting burned by the exhaust system."

Pete opens the hydraulic valve on the spreader, and the car begins to rise slowly. The crew of Hazmat 6, Robert, Fred and Tony jump into action .Fred begins to deploy the air bags, compressor, and hoses while Robert tries to start the compressor.

Eric, "put two air bags in the back driver's side Fred. Joe, get ready when the car goes up far enough pull him out! Now get more cribbing ready."

Just as the car begins to lift off of the boy's body, and Joe reaches in under the car, Mike screams out, "The wood is cracking!"

With a loud crack, the wood splits and the entire weight of the car comes crashing down on the boy and the upper body of paramedic Joe Garcia, who had put his own life in danger by going under the car to keep traction on the boys neck while the other firefighter pulled the boys feet. The teenage girl who had been driving the car hears the loud noise, turns around to see what happened, and passes out.

The boy's parents, seeing all the commotion, arrive from the other end of the park. Upon seeing the bike and a red tennis shoe protruding from under the car, the father yells out, "Johnny!"

He immediately dives in to try to pull his son from under the wreckage. The police try to restrain the hysterical mother and crazed father; who is trying to lift the car off his son. The mother turns to the crowd and yell out,"Help us please, help."

The bystanders, who have gathered at the scene, push through the cops and jump in to help. Even though this is against departmental protocol, the firefighters and all the men grab hold of the vehicle and try to lift one end.

"Alright, on three, everybody lift!"

With a mighty heave, one end of the vehicle comes off the ground. Joe and the lifeless body of the boy are pulled from under the wreckage.

Joe is shaken by his near miss but has sustained only minor injuries to his face and right arm.

"Joe, are you alright?" Bert asks him.

"Yeah, I'm fine, don't worry about me. Take care of the boy."

Tommy the other paramedic franticly works on the boy. Bert calls in Rescue 3 to dispatch.

"Rescue 3 QSK,"

"Dispatch, can you contact metro on status of Air One?"

"Rescue 3, 122 has already called for Air One. They are en route."

"QSL, have them come to the east end of the park. Engine 5 is setting up a landing zone now."

Tommy, "Bert, he has no pulse, and his neck is broken!"

Bert puts down his radio and examines the lifeless little body on the ground.

Tommy, "He's gone, what are we going to do, we can't fly out a dead person."

"I know, I know! Load him into the rescue truck."

"Rescue 3 to dispatch." QSK Rescue 3, "dispatch 07 Air One."

"122 to Rescue 3." QSK 122, "Bert are you sure that you want to cancel Air One?"

"QSL, chief the boy is gone Sir!"

Upon hearing this over the radio, Eric comes running over.

"Bert, what are you doing?"

"I'm following protocol, Eric. We evacuate victims. We do not evacuate bodies!"

"But what if you're wrong Bert."—like you were in making that call on the spreader Eric?"

"I did what I thought was right at the time to save a boy's life!"

Bert, "Yeah, and in so doing you put Joe's life in danger, I will transport the boy to the Hialeah Hospital and let them pronounce him dead there!"

"Rescue 3 to dispatch." "QSK Rescue 3." "Rescue 3 transporting one to Hialeah Hospital!"

"Bert, what the hell do I tell the parents?"

"I don't know, Eric!"

Eric now turns to the father, who is beating his hands against the hood of the car that took his boy's life.

"Where are they taking my boy? He's going to be alright, isn't he?"

"Sir, I have, I mean, we did all that we could."

The mother, hearing this, walks over to Eric and grabs his turnout gear. She yells, "you are the reason my boy is dead! You dropped the car on my little Johnny!"

Eric turns and slowly walks away.

"You will have to sleep, knowing you killed my son! Why? Why did you do it?"

Mike comes up behind him.

"We all know you were only trying to save him. She'll come to her senses."

Eric, "Yeah, and I almost got Joe killed, too!"

All the gear is loaded back into the trucks and the men get back into their units and return to their stations. As the men of ladder 3 ride back to the station, the mood in the truck is a somber one. After what seamed like a long ride they are back at the station.

"Ladder 3 in quarters"

Dispatch, "QSL Ladder 3."

Eric, "Mike, Can you guys clean up without me?"

"Yeah, boss. We got it. You take care of your paperwork."

"Thanks. Yeah, by the way, thanks, guys —you did a great job out there today."

Pete replies, "Just another day in the life of a ladder man, boys!"

"So, I can see a pay increase in my next check?" He adds sensing the need to lighten the mood.

Mike says, "Paycheck? I thought you paid us to sleep here, Pete!"

Pete, "Very funny, guys. You have no idea how difficult it is to be a ladder man at this station, with all the pressure and no rookies to pick up the slack.

Pete, "By the way rookie this is your first incident, so you have to by ice cream for the men today."

Pete, "When do you think we are going to get a permanent rookie for our station?"

Bert, "What are you looking for—a new boyfriend Pete?"

"Maybe Howe's butt is beginning to sag a little, and he's looking a little rough around the edges?"

Howe, "Yeah, well, it's not easy to get out of a lounge chair three times a day at my age, I wonder who it will be at your age Pete?"

"Funny, Howe!"

Eric, "Okay, you guys, you work out all the problems at the station. I'm going to call Barbie."

Howe, "Hey, Mike, do you think he'll catch some flak from the chief for that call?"

"I hope not, Howe. His only thoughts were to save that boy."

Mike, "I'm glad I didn't have to make that call!"

Howe, "Pete, is that why you never took the lieutenant's test?"

Mike, "Nah, Pete could never stay awake for more than two hours at a time, Howe."

Pete, "That's because Mike's old lady kept me up all night."

Mike, "Yeah, well, serves you right for looking at a naked picture of her before you go to bed!"

Howe, "Is she that ugly, Pete?"

Pete, "You ever see a shaved ape, Howe?"

"No."

Pete, "Hey, Mike, Howe wants to see a picture of your old lady."

Mike, "Okay, but don't come crying in the morning if you can't sleep tonight?"

In the other room Eric close the door. He reaches for the phone to call the person he has turned to since they we teens. "Hey, Barbie, how are you doing?"

"I'm okay. I heard the news about the boy. It must have been awful."

"How did you find out so fast?"

"Tony called his wife from the hazmat truck, and she called me. Is Joe going to be alright?"

"Uh-huh, Joe's going to be fine."

Think this would be a good time to cheer him up with her news.

"Eric, I have some great news!" She says excitedly.

"Go ahead Barbie; I could use some good news."

"My manager got a call from the record company. They liked my demo, and they want to see and hear me perform it for them in Los Angeles."

"Baby, that's the best news I've heard all day."

Just then Chief Daniels walks into the room.

Daniels, "Eric in my quarters!"

"Yes sir, chief."

"I have to go Barbie. I'll call you later."

"Is there something wrong, Eric?"

"No."

"Is that Chief Daniels? He sounded angry. Did something happen, Eric?"

"It's fine. I'll call you soon Barbie."

Daniels, "Eric, in my quarters now!" The chief shout from down the hall.

Eric hangs the phone up.

As Eric enters his quarters, the chief explodes.

"Lieutenant, what the hell was that?! You ignored protocol and used the spreader to lift a car?"

"Yes, but chief I."

"Don't 'but chief me.' You ride acting captain for one day, and you decide to rewrite the book on extrication."

"If I may Chief—"

"No, you may not! The jaws are for cutting, and the spreader is for opening jammed doors, not lifting cars off people!"

"Sir, I know how to use the jaws!"

"Do you, Lieutenant?"

Chief," The cities spends five thousand dollars on air bag system that can lift an entire railroad car off the ground and you decide to use the spreaders instead."

Eric," Sir the compressor for the air bags has been acting up, and we were running out of time."

"Lieutenant, what you have done is open the city up to a possible lawsuit. Do you have any idea how many lawyers are out there right now trying to contact those parents?"

"Sir, we did the best we could to save that child. Joe risked his life to save him."

"Yes, I know you put Joe's life on the line too. Do you have any idea what it costs this city to put a medic through school?"

"No, I have no idea how much money it takes. All I know is there is no amount of money that mother would have taken in exchange for her child's life, and we did our absolute best under the circumstances."

"Save it for the jury, Lieutenant!"

"Sir, I did what I considered appropriate at the time."

"Appropriate, Lieutenant?"

"Yes, sir!"

"When you are the top-ranking officer at the scene, the first and most appropriate action involves ensuring the safety of your men!"

"With all due respect, chief, you were on the scene and you did not take over."

"What the hell are you trying to say, Eric? Are you inferring that I'm afraid to do my job?"

"That's not what I—"

"Get the hell out of my quarters! We're done here, Lieutenant!"

Eric walks out closing the door behind him; he can hear the chief pick up his phone and begin dialing.

The men heard the chief yelling even with the close door and they are all waiting in the kitchen for Eric.

Mike, "Eric, how did it go with the old man?"

"Not now, Mike!"

"Hey, we were all thinking of the boy and his family. Anyone in your position would have done the same thing, Eric."

"Yeah, but I'm the one who made the call and risked Joe's life for a boy who was probably already dead."

13

Mike, "Eric, no one knew for sure he was dead, and something had to be done."

"I guess Mike. I just wish it had been someone else."

"You knew when you put those gold bars on your collar that these calls would come up. You did the right thing Eric, and we all know it."

"Tell it to those parents in the park. Mike, I got tunnel vision, and you know that can get you killed or, worse, your crew! The chief is right—I didn't use my head. I threw all my training out the window!"

Mike, "The chief! What kind of call do you think he would have made?"

Mike, "Fred Smart was a rookie and Daniels was a lieutenant, and he would ask Fred for advice on a rescue call."

Mike, "Yeah, can you believe Daniels was once a paramedic?"

Pete, "That's a scary thought!"

Pete, "Hell, Fred Smart on B shift was at Station Four with him one day when Daniels was a lieutenant and they got a call of a house fire. Daniels forgot to load his fire boots on the truck. So, what does he do? He reaches back through the cab widow and pulls Fred's boots from Fred's gear and puts them on."

"Fred is still on probation and now he thinks he lost his boots. Can you imagine being a rooky fireman and showing up at a house fire in tennis shoes?"

Pete, "In my book, Daniels was and still is an idiot!"

Eric, "He is, Pete, but he is still the idiot in charge."

THE HIALEAH FIRE department has three shifts A, B, and C. the stations have the same amount of men per station per shift.

The next morning as C shift goes off duty and A shift comes on duty.

A shift lieutenant Cliff Adams "Morning, Eric, were you guys busy yesterday?"

"Yeah!" Eric walks out without saying another word.

Cliff, "What's up with him?"

Bill Thomson A shift fireman. "Didn't you hear about the boy in the park yesterday?"

Cliff, "No, what happened?"

Firefighter Bill, "See if you guys lived in the city, like you are supposed to, you would know these events."

Cliff, "The only reason you live in the city, Bill, is because you still live with your mommy!" Just then Bert walks in. Cliff "So what happened at the park Bert what are they talking about here?"

Bert, "I really rather not talk about it now"

Outside Eric runs into Joe as he is putting his gear away.

Eric, "Hey, man, you okay?"

"Sure, I'm a little sore, but I'll be fine." "My tennis game may be off for a few days, but I'll survive."

"Joe, I'm sorry!"

"Eric, nobody told me to get under that car—that's all on me."

"Thanks, Joe, but I still feel responsible for what happened."

Their conversation is interrupted by the station PA system. The chief summons Joe into his office.

"Joe, come see me in my office before you go home"

Joe rolls his eyes, "I'll talk to later Eric"

In the chiefs office. "Yes sir, Chief!"

Joe, "Did you write an accident report when you got back?"

"No, I didn't think—"

Chief, "You didn't think? We had a lot of that going on around here yesterday, before you leave, I want that report to go in today's mail downtown."

"I'm on it, chief!"

As he walks to his truck Eric sees the chief walking toward him.

Chief, "Lieutenant, we will talk about this next duty day."

"Yes sir chief."

He sits in his truck and as he looks at the steering wheel he wounder if he made the correct choice in choosing this career.

On the way home, Eric has to pass by the park. He knows he has to let go and treat each incident without getting emotionally involved. It is the only way to do his job and retain his sanity. However, he finds that the steering wheel turns and it takes the truck into the park, as if someone else is driving. Now, he is at the scene again.

Flowers have been placed where the boy laid. He slowly gets out and walks over to them, as the events of the day before are played over in his mind. He bends down and touches one of the yellow roses placed where the boy's body had come to rest. As he picks up the flowers, all covered in last night's dew, they appear to be weeping at the tragic loss of a life so young—cut short in such a tragic way. He now finds a tear running down his own cheek.

Again and again he runs through the events in his mind, one by one. He wonders what he could have done differently. Woundering if he could have done it any different and would it have had a different outcome? With a start, he comes back to reality with the ringing of his cell phone.

"Hello Baby!"

"Where are you Eric? You're late!"

"I'm sorry Barbie. I'll be there in a few."

"Eric, don't forget that you need to take Maxx to the vet today to have the stitches removed."

"I know I'm on my way back now."

He slowly places the flowers back where he found them and gets back in his truck. He takes one last look at the flowers, puts the truck in gear, and drives away.

When he arrives home, he sees Maxx at the back gate, tail wagging, greeting him with his usual low growl.

Eric opens the backyard gate, "What do you say, Maxx? I'm happy to see you, too." He makes his way to the backyard door, unlocking it. "Hi Barbie".

From inside the house, Barbie speaks.

"Hey, baby, I'm running late for work. What happened? Where did you go? Mike Campos from Station 6 called. He was looking for you. He told me everything. Are you going to be alright?"

Being the kind of man that he is, and not wanting to worry her.

"Yeah I'm fine Barbie, You go on to work, and we'll talk when you get home."

Barbie, "Okay, love you!"

"Me, too!"

"Oh, you love you too?"

"You know what I mean, Barbie!"

"I know Eric, later!"

Eric sits at the dinner table and looks at the picture on the wall of him, Mikey, Bert and the rest of his graduating firefighter's class and he remembers how much fun they had and how they thought they would make the best fireman ever.

Then the sound of the house phone brings him back.

"Hey, Mikey, I was getting ready to call you back?"

"I heard about the park thing, I'm sorry it turned into such a mess Eric"

"Thanks, it's all part of the game. What's on your mind Mike?"

"Well, if you can break away from Barbie for two weeks, I'm going to take the old thirty-five-footer on a sailing trip from here to the Bahamas. Then I'll go on down to Costa Rica for some fabulous fishing, aged rum, crystal-clear waters, and beautiful women—or men, in your case! Well, what do you say?"

"I don't know, Mike. It sounds good, but let me think it over and talk with Barbie. I'll let you know."

Mikey, "Talk it over? I told Jill I was going, and that's it!"

"Was she in the room when you said it Mike?"

"No, but if she had been ... you know I'm the head of this family!"

"I know you are the head ... and she's the body that tells you which way to look and where to go!"

"Yeah, but I'm still the head! Okay, dude? Don't take too long, I already have a list of boys who want to come along."

Eric, "Boys, yeah, but how many men?"

"Yeah, mister macho man! Hey, how is Maxx doing?"

"He's good. The stitches come out today."

"Eric you need to stop that hog hunting. I know those hogs coast your buddy Keith a lot of money with the damage they do to the crops and the cattle pastures, but one day you're both going to get cut up."

"Now you sound like Barbie!"

"Well, with that beautiful voice of hers, I'll take that as a compliment. How is her singing career coming along?"

Eric, "She has good news on that. I'll know more later."

"Good luck. She deserves a break after putting up with the likes of you Eric."

"I love you too, Mike!"

"Later! And, remember Eric, there is a list!"

"But I'm still number one, right?"

"Indeed, you are, man!"

"Thanks, Mikey. Bye!"

WEDNESDAY, B SHIFT IS GOING OFF DUTY AND C IS COMING ON DUTY WITH ITS REGULAR CREW AND CAPTAIN ED MATHEWS BACK ON THE LADDER.

Captain Ed walks into the duty office.

B shift Captain Otto, "Hey, Ed, looks like you can't take a day off without the station going all to hell!"

Ed, "Why? What happened? Did Pete lock the rookie out of the station again?"

"No, Ed you haven't heard?"

"No, did my ladder truck break down again?"

Otto "No, they had a bad one at Milander Park, and your beloved chief had a cow."

"What went wrong Otto?"

Just then the Chief Daniels walks in.

Ed, "Ah, hey! Good morning, Chief!"

"Morning men! Ed, after roll call I need to speak with you in my quarters."

"Sure. Before or after PT?"

Chief, "Before!"

Eric walks in the duty room.

"Good morning, Ed."

"Hey, morning, Eric!"

Eric, "Morning, Chief."

The chief keeps looking at the duty line up for the day and says nothing.

Chief, "When you're done here, Ed."

Ed, "Hey, Eric, can you finish roll call for me?"

"Sure Ed!"

They walk into the chief's quarters. Chief, "close the door Ed".

18

"Ed, I guess you heard what happened at the park on Sunday?"

"As a matter of fact, chief I don't have a clue. Otto was in the process of telling me."

"I'm not going into the long or short of it Ed. I'm going to write up Lieutenant Eric Montana for not following procedure."

"Chief, he's one of the best young lieutenants we have."

Chief, "He used the spreader to lift a car off a child, and it fell back on the child and on one of our men, Joe."

"What happened to the child chief?"

"He was dead, rescue 3 took him to the hospital so they colud pronounced him dead there. We thought that would be best for the parent's sake."

"How about Joe was he hurt?"

"He was slightly injured."

Ed, "Where was hazmat?"

"They were there, but Eric claims the compressor for the air bags was not working properly."

"Chief, not being there, I can't second-guess Eric."

"I was there, and it was a bad call. I'm not asking your advice or permission. As second in command here, I just want you to be aware of what is going to happen."

"Have you talked to our battalion chief yet, chief?"

"No, George was off duty. I will be speaking to him later."

"Is that it, Chief?"

"Yeah, we're done, Captain."

Ed leaves the chief's quarters and walks out to the engine bay were all the men are all waiting for him.

Ed", Ok, are you ladies ready for a little basketball?"

"Bert, where is Joe today?" Eric asks.

"He's at Station 2. He'll be riding lieutenant today."

Eric, "Have you spoken to him today?"

"No, but I called him at home yesterday, and he was fine."

"Bert, "you know how tough we rescue men are, right?"

Pete says, "Oh, yes, you guys are regular gladiators. You like wearing short pants and bathing with young boys!"

Cliff, "So, I see you're not on the ladder truck today, Pete."

"Yeah, the rookie has to take some kind of test, and I am stuck on the fire truck until after lunch."

Cliff, "I think we'll do fire training all morning, so Pete can remember how it feels to be a real firefighter!"

Ladder 3's Captain Ed Mathews interjects. "Don't worry. Pete." You'll be back with the real men after lunch.

Pete, "But you know, Ed, bad company can ruin good morals!"

Cliff says, "Let's go to PT. Maybe we can find you some morals on the way, Pete?"

Mike says, "Those were very profound words, Pete! Have you been reading Shakespeare?"

"No, that's from the bible!"

"You're not going to tell me you've been reading the bibles now are you Pete?"

Cliff says, "Pete didn't read the bible. He was there with Moses when God gave him the Ten Commandments!"

Pete replies, "You should look this good when you get to be my age!"

Mike asks, "Has anyone seen Eric?"

"He's calling downtown to see if there is any vacation time available."

Cliff asks, "Ed, how did it go with Daniels"

"You know him. This is just another excuse for him to be at City Hall and brown-nose the brass!"

Cliff, "What about, George, Ed you think he'll come down hard on Eric?"

"I don't think he will. You know he is still a fireman at heart, unlike our chief Daniels and our beloved head chief Magee."

"I still can't believe how our big boss chief Magee takes the mayor's side over us every time." "Pete, you and Magee came on together right?" "No, actually he came on later Cliff." Pete says as he shakes his head.

Bert, "You guys forget Pete was a fireman on the Mayflower when it landed on Plymouth Rock!"

Mike says, "I heard when Pete first came on, they would pee on their loincloths, then stomp out the fire with it!"

Pete says, "You can laugh all you want, but when I came on men were men and sheep knew it! Just ask Cliff's mom!"

Cliff says, "Thaaat's nooot fuuunny!

Eric grabs the two way radio, "Are you men ready to ride?"

"Sure, let's go!"

On a typical duty day at PT you would have at least two different stations at one of the city parks. In so doing the number of trucks at one park could sometimes be as many as six, each with three man crews. The city is also broken into two sections with one district chief for the south with the call numbers 121 and 122 for the north end, a battalion chief over the entire city for each shift 103, and the chief of the entire department for all shifts 101.

Ed says, "Ladder 3, Engine 3, will be 09 PT Milander Park for PT."

"Dispatch, QSL Ladder 3 and Engine 3."

"Engine 6 and hazmat 6 will be 09 PT Milander Park for PT."

"103 will be 09 to Milander for PT."

"Why do you think Battalion chief 103 is going to drive all the way here to do PT with us?"

"You know George—he loves his basketball."

"Yeah, Ed, but he has lost to the guys at Station 1. Plus, they always play at Sparks Park against Engine 4."

"I bet Lt. Randy is going to be pissed if he doesn't have enough for a three on three basketball game."

"Randy has Jim Wright. He can be the third man."

"You know Jim— his idea of PT is talking about alimony, NASCAR, and how the minorities are taking over the country. He has to be the most miserable person to walk into a fire station!"

They are all talking as they make their way to the basketball courts. The rookie, walking a few steps behind them, hears the conversation about Jim and gives them a piece of information that makes the whole group stop and break down.

Rookie, "Guys, I was stationed at 4 with Jim two weeks ago, and his new girlfriend came over to the station. You guys know she works at Wal-Mart. Well, last Wednesday, I was riding my bicycle around the lake and she was sitting in her station wagon with some black dude."

Cliff, "Hey, Louie, you hear that?"

Louie, "O man, I can't wait to see him at the grocery store today!"

Ed, "here comes George."

"Morning, ladies!"

Ed, "Hey, boss!"

Ed says, "Now, you know this is not going to be like playing the geriatric crews you usually face at the south end?" George, "I will keep that in mind."

After the game, George walks over to Eric.

"I need to talk to you a minute Lt."

"Yes sir."

"First thing, you called for vacation. I will look at the roster and see what I can do, when I get back to the station."

"Thanks, George."

"Second, I already got an earful from Daniels on the events of Sunday. You know I always back my men when I can, and my response to him was to let this go. But, you know him when he has an agenda; he doesn't care who he steps on to get there."

Eric' "I know and chief Magee is no better, he sees everything from the Mayors point of view."

"George, you are the best man to become the next top chief of the whole department, so why won't you take it?"

"Bite your tongue. I thought you liked me, Eric."

"Come on, boss, you're the best man to lead this department."

"And spend my days in the mayor's office! Thanks, but no thanks!"

Eric, "You know, boss, women like a man in a suit and tie."

"Suit and tie! I can just see myself now, walking into the mayor's office in a suit and tie and my flip flops! On this time-off thing, are you thinking of going sailing with Mikey?"

"I am considering it. But Barbie has an opportunity to sing for this record label, and she has to fly out to Los Angeles. I don't want her to fly out there by herself. I need to back here in time for her"

George, "Well, I could always go with her for you!"

"You and half the department! Thanks, boss!"

"All kidding aside, I will call you later and let you know if those days are available."

"Thanks, George. Oh, by the way, did you hear about Jim's latest girlfriend?"

Just then the two way radio comes on with a message for chief George.

Dispatch to 103, "101 would like to speak with you as soon as possible chief." George, "103 QSL, I will call the 101 as soon as I am back in quarters"

"Don't worry, Eric, you made a call. It didn't have the outcome you would have liked, but you did your best and that's all anyone can do."

"Thanks, George, but this does eat away at me. You ever make a call you wish you could re-call, George?"

"Oh, yeah, but we're divorced now! Don't let this get to you, kid. You are one hell of a fireman, and one day you will look back at this and realize there was nothing you could have done to change the outcome. And, as for making a mistake, yes, I was a *swing* lieutenant. It was my second month as lieutenant out of Station 1.

When a firefighter is promoted to a higher rank they must ride at different stations to cover for absent personal in the position they haves been promoted to .Engineers, lieutenants, and captains will swing from station to station, until they can get a permanent station.

"I was assigned to Station 2. I remember we had just finished wiping down the engine for the night, when we heard the call come in for Engine 2 and Rescue 2. It was a hot muggy night and the date was July third. Two families were headed home on East Fourth. They were on their way home from the grocery store with a car full of groceries in anticipation of the annual family picnic at Madison Hammocks Beach the next day. The occupants were two pregnant females in their late twenties, their respective husbands, and a six-year-old female. Their car was hit by a southbound car that ran the light. It hit the rear passenger side and sent the car into such a violent spin that the driver's side passenger door opened, sending the two pregnant females and the little girl flying out.

"Rescue was on its way back from transporting a patient to Hialeah Hospital, so they were the first to arrive. They immediately called for Ladder 1, the district chief, and our truck to set up a landing zone for

Metro Air One to land. Rescue 2's lieutenant informed us, over the radio that they had passed a slow-moving train headed north and we needed to either move fast or take the 21st Street overpass because the train could cut us off. I had Larry Jones driving. He was going to make a U-turn and go for a sure clear passage over the overpass, but I told him I thought we could make it before the train. George puts his hand on Eric's shoulder. You know that felling you get in your stomach when you know you screwed up."

"Yes sir I do."

"Well Larry didn't say a word. He didn't have to. His expression said it for him. To make a long story short, we did not beat the train and lost precious time driving back taking the overpass."

"When we arrived it looked like a scene from a Hollywood movie. There was oil and radiator fluid everywhere. Whit lots of scattered soda cans, some intact and some already exploded, along with canned foods and hundreds of pieces of watermelon. You know, I still can't eat watermelon without thinking of that incident. We began to set up the LZ in the middle of the intersection as usual, but in our haste, we did not realize the potential danger from all those cans becoming flying projectiles. Luckily, Tommy Steel kicked a can out of his way and realized if we tried to land the chopper in the middle of that intersection we would have flying projectiles going everywhere. We were able to reroute the chopper at the last minute.

Eric, "Did you catch any flak from the chief?"

The only thing the district chief 122 said after the chopper took off and all the rescue trucks left, was, "George, as a rookie lieutenant, you have to go for ice cream for your station *after* your first major incident, not before you get there."

Eric, "who was 122 that day?"

"It was David Mac."

"Did you ever work with him, Eric?"

"A couple of times after he made battalion chief on A shift."

George, "Back then, we were more concerned with fighting fire and saving lives than with playing politicians!"

"Good ole days, huh, boss?"

"Yeah Eric they sure were!"

George, "Well, as for Magee and your incident, I don't think he will push the issue. I'll call you later and let you know if I can get you those days off and if there is any more on this issue."

"Thanks, boss!"

BACK AT STATION # 3 THE ENGINE CREW IS BACK IN QUARTERS, AS ERIC AND HIS MEN MAKE PREPERATION TO GO OUT AND DO BUILING INSECTIONS.

Mike, "Okay, rookie, what are you going to cook for us tonight?"

"Well, I can grill some burgers."

"Did you say hamburgers?"

"Yes, sir hamburgers and corn!"

Mike, "I think we have another mama's boy here who doesn't know how to cook."

"Hey, Cliffy, you teach at the fire college. Don't you screen these guys to see if they can cook before you send them out as rookies?"

"Pete, the only screening Cliffy does is in the showers."

Cliff responds, "Well, he can't cook, is terrible at basketball, and he got here late on his first day! I think he'll be perfect on the ladder crew!"

Pete: "Hey, Howe, what do you think? Shall we put this new guy on the ladder?"

"Over my dead body! He rides rescue first, then the engine, and if I die, then he goes on the ladder!"

Rescue 3 arrives from transporting a patient to Hialeah Hospital.

As Bert, Rescue 3's lieutenant, gets out of the truck, he sees Eric standing next to the hose rack talking with the men.

"Got a minute, Eric?"

"Sure, Bert."

"We just got back from Hialeah Hospital, and I spoke with the trauma surgeon on duty last Sunday. He told me the boy was probably dead before we even got to Milander Park; his neck was broken in three places."

"Thanks, Bert."

"Don't sweat it, man. Hey, are you going on Mike's sailing trip?"

"The more I think about it, the better it sounds, Bert."

Bert, "I hear that. If I could get the time off, I would definitely go too."

Rooky opens the station door and shouts out. "Alright, men, lunch is on!"

"Okay, let's eat."

Just then, the PA comes to life.

"Rescue 3, 3-42 elderly women hit by a car, west end parking lot of Wal-Mart."

Bert, "Here we go again! Rescue 3 responding."

No more is said about Sunday's incident for the reminder of the day.

Pulling into his front yard the next morning, Eric sees Maxx sitting by the chain-link fence. His big brown eyes sparkle in the early morning sun.

"Hi, big guy, did you take good care of my girl?"

Maxx walks the length of the fence, leaning his muscular body against it, making his usual low grumbling.

"Speak up, Maxx,"

"Grow, wow, wow!"

"Alright, I'll take that as a yes, and we can talk later, big guy."

He tiptoes inside and makes his way to the bedroom. He slowly gets into bed and gently reaches over and kisses Barbie's forehead.

"Wake up, sleepy head."

Barbie, "Hi, baby, how was your night?"

"It was good. Only one call all night. Did you hear anything from Karl on the Los Angeles gig?"

"They called and want us there September fifteenth. I looked at your schedule and you will be off on RDO starting the seventeenth. Karl is going to call them today and explain how an RDO works and see if they will move it up two days."

Eric, "Good, if I can't go, I know your mom will go for sure".

"Why won't you be able to go Eric? You know this means a lot to me you."

"I didn't say I would not go Barbie, I only said if."

"Javy and I are going to take the dogs out for a run tomorrow at West T'S ranch with Keith."

"Eric, please don't put Maxx out. His side is still not healed, and don't let Keith drive"

"Just because that tree jumped out in front of Keith that one time."

"One time Eric he drives that truck like he is in the Indy 500."

He gives her a big smile. "Don't worry baby, we'll be alright."

NEXT DAY

The alarm goes off. Its four A.M. Eric quietly puts on his jeans, slips into his boots, and tries to make his way out of the room without waking Barbie. As he slowly closes the door behind him, she wakes.

"Be careful. I love you!"

"Love you too, baby!"

He goes outside and taps on Javy's window.

Javy's radio is blasting.

"Javy, turn that radio down, man. It's four A.M.!"

"Hey, man, that's 'Amarillo by Morning' by the man, George Straight. Reminds me of my rodeo days."

"Javy, riding a bowlegged milk cow named Buttercup at your uncle's two-acre farm is not exactly pro rodeo!"

"Have you forgotten my ride at the Davie amateur bull-rider event?"

"Sure, you got on the bull, he jumped left, and you went right!"

"True! But, do you remember the way the girls all looked at me when we got to the bar?"

"Javier, you landed on a pile of bull manure. Everybody in that place was looking at you! They all wanted to see which way you were going, so they could go the other way." Eric teases his childhood friend.

"True, but they did look."

Javy, "Butterscotch!"

"What Javy?"

"Butterscotch. That was the name of the cow!"

"Oh, I'm sorry, Javy. Butterscotch sounds so much more intimidating than Buttercup." They both laugh.

"You and Barbie want to go to the bar tonight with me and Heather? You know they'll love to have her sing."

"Maybe, but you know she only knows a couple of country songs."

"She can sing that song from *Titanic*. They loved it last time she sang it."

"We'll see. Let's ride!"

"Eric, are you taking Maxx?"

"Yeah, he needs the exercise. Javy, aslo I need to be back early."

"No problem I'll only buy twenty four pack of beer for Keith then."

"Hey, Javy, would you like to go on a sailing trip with me and some of the guys?"

"Where to?"

"The Bahamas and then Costa Rica."

"How long are you going to be out?"

"About two days at the Bahamas and the rest fishing in Costa Rica. About three weeks total."

"I have one week of vacation. I could fly out to the Bahamas and then fly back from Costa Rica."

"I'll talk to Mikey to see if he has the room. Remind me, and I'll call Mike later."

Later that day, Barbie gets a phone call.

"Hi, doll face."

"Hi, Karl, what's new?"

"I spoke with the producers. I explained to them how your boyfriend works one day on then two off, and after doing this six times in a row, he then gets five days off. This being his RDO, Barbie, they agreed to move your demo up two days so he can accompany you."

"Thanks, Karl!"

"You know, Barbie, you can't build your career around his RDOs or his vacation time. You need a man who can be there for you twenty-four-seven and preferably someone with my contacts in the industry. Eric is a nice guy, if you're looking for someone in jeans and cowboy boots for a fun weekend. You need a steady man with a plan in your life."

"We have been down this road before, Karl. You know I appreciate everything you've done for me, but there is only one man in my life, and that's Eric."

"Then when is he going to ask you to marry him?"

"I have to go now, Karl."

"Okay, but remember I'm here, ready, and willing to marry you tomorrow. Oh, one last thing—have you given any more thought to changing you name?"

"I like my name, and, besides, my dad will most likely have a fit if I change it."

"If you are serious about your career, you need to listen to me, or else we are both wasting our time."

"What did you have in mind, Karl?"

"Well, I'm thinking you should go with one name."

"You mean like Cher or Madonna?"

"Something like that. Barbie I was thinking something like Opel, Crystal, or Safire."

"Let me think about it and talk it over with Eric."

"Here we go again. Is Eric in the business or am I?"

"You're in the business, but he's in my heart, and I like to consult with him too, Karl."

"Fine. Barbie Bye!"

Eric phones Mike from the woods.

"Hey, Mikey, what's up, can you talk?"

"Yea!"

"Do you have room on that sailboat for one more?"

"Well, so far it's just you and me, Eric."

"What happened to the long list of guys that wanted to go?"

"I think they're afraid of that depression building off the coast of Africa."

"What depression, Mike?"

"It's some small depression. It's small now, and I don't think it will come to much. Besides, the computer forecasts take it out to sea."

"Are you a meteorologist now Mike?"

"No, but I'm sure we'll be fine."

29

"I'm not sailing into any depression, Mike."

"Not to worry, who is your fearless seafaring captain?"

"Okay, fearless, but I'm telling you, I'm not sailing into any hurricane!"

Mike, "this thing will be gone by the time we get to the Bahamas."

"I hope so. Talk at you later, Mikey."

"Bye, Eric."

Eric hangs up the phone.

"Do you still want to go, Javy?"

Javy puts his arm around Eric "Sure, if you go, I'll go bud."

That night, Eric walks into the house in time to overhear Barbie talking on the phone to her dad.

"But, Dad, I will still have my name. Most entertainers have stage names ... No; I haven't discussed it with Eric."

Eric says, "Discuss what?"

"I'll talk to you later Daddy, I love you!" She hangs up.

"Talk to me about what?"

"Karl wants me to get a stage name."

"What's wrong with your name?"

"Now you sound like my dad. Karl thinks a single name would help me with the young crowd."

"What does he know about the young crowd? He's thirty-five years old!"

"Eric, he knows, that's his job."

"The only reason he got that job is because his daddy has money and knew a few people from back in his pot-smoking days."

"Regardless, he got them to move the rehearsal date up so you can come."

"I bet Karl's happy about that!"

"Stop it, Eric!"

"Stop what? I see the way he looks at you. If he weren't your manager, I would have kicked his ass from here to Key West."

"Well, you can put and end to that."

"Yeah, how?"

"Make me Mrs. Eric Montana, You have been a part of me half my life, we have been engaged and living together now for almost two years."

"You know I love you, Barbie, but you also know I want to have enough for a house before we get married."

"Eric, all I need is you. We can buy a house later. Besides, if my singing takes off, we will have enough to buy two houses."

"I can see it now. The guys in the department would ride me like a bowlegged pony at a birthday party. No, thanks! I'll buy our first home. Then, if or when your career takes off, you can buy that second home."

"If I make it big, you could just give up the job and travel with me."

"Give up my job? Never. That's who I am and will always be!"

"Eric, I can't build my career around your RDOs."

"No, you can't, can you? Maybe you need someone like Karl? With his smooth talking and all those connections that are so important to your future."

"The most important thing in my life is you, Eric!"

"I know. Let's drop this for now."

"Okay."

"Listen, Mikey invited me on a sailing trip to the Bahamas and Costa Rica."

"How many days?"

"He was talking three weeks, but if there's a storm out there, we would have to cut it short, either way I will be back to make the tripe to LA with you."

"Eric, please don't go out if the weather is bad. You have the rest of your life to take these trips. Don't take any chances please!"

"I won't, and we'll be fine."

"Eric, does that mean you're going?"

"I would like to go. I need to get away from the job for a while and think."

"Do you need to get away from me too, Eric?"

"No, never. But, I do have a lot on my mind right now, Barbie."

"What about me? You don't think I have a lot on my mind too? Karl says if I don't get my career off the ground now, it might never happen."

"I don't want to talk about Karl anymore! Come on, let's go out to eat."

"But I have everything ready to cook."

"What were you going to cook?"

"Your favorite."

"Seafood soup?"

"Yep!"

"Alright, let's cook."

She closes the refrigerator door and turns. In front of her is Eric, he has the faucet running and is staring out the window a lost look on his face.

She walks up behind him wraps her arms around him. "Go with Mike, I'll be fine and we can make the trip to LA when you get back."

He turns around and they kiss. "You sure you'll be allright; I can fly back with Javy if we take longer than expected."

"Yes, I'll be fine, but promise me if the storm intensifies, or heads your way you will not continue the trip and come home to me."

"It's a deal, now let me peel some of those shrimp."

Just then the phone rings. "Hi Mike, what's up?"

"Did Barbie give you permission to go, or do I have to go over there and beg her to let you go?"

"Funny you should call now; we were just talking about that."

"Well what's the verdict, can you go or not?"

"We're good; she and I only have one concerned, that storm, I don't like the thought of being out there in the middle of a hurricane."

"Forget that little storm and listen to this."

"Little storm, Mike?" Eric exclaims.

Barbie slaps the counter with her hands. "Did he just say little storm? I swear you guys are like little kids, when you get an idea in your heads, no amount of common sense can make you change your minds."

'Did you hear what Barbie just said Mike?"

"Yes I did but, Eric relaxes a minute and let me talk, I spoke with Gus on B shift, his parents have a vacation home in Costa Rica, and he said we can use it while we are there. Now picture this, a two story house on the ocean with a balcony that looks out over the ocean."

"That's great news. It would be nice to have a nice hot bath, and be able to sleep in something bigger than a bunk bed for a day or two."

"The best part of all this is, and tells Barbie this, we are not paying a penny for any of this, and we can just call it off at any time, if the weather changes on us."

"Is this a done deal Mike, or are you two just talking?"

"It's a done deal, He will bring me the key next duty day and we'll be all set."

"Sounds too good to pass up, I'm in for sure and so is Javy, I'll talk to you later Mike, bye."

"Bye Eric."

In light of this good news, the storm and all the dangers it can bring are momentarly forgotten. Eric thoughts turn to getting away from the job for a while hoping maybe things will have changed when he gets back. Little does he know that the biggest change in his life is only days away. A change that will test his love for Barbie, and her commitment to the only man she has ever loved.

Chapter Three
The Storm

Two days later, Eric is at the marina at six A.M. The sun is slowly rising as if it were magically coming out of the middle of Atlantic Ocean. Its rays dance across the sea's surface from wave to wave, sending rays of light in all directions. He watches a flock of seagulls as they shake off the night's long sleep and make their way out to sea for their daily feed. As their shapes fade into the horizon, his thoughts turn back to Barbie and all that is going on between them. He can't help but wonder what the future will hold for them.

He turns his attention to the bay. It looks like a large bowl of emerald Jell-O, like someone could actually walk on its surface. He pulls into a spot next to Mikey, who is unloading groceries.

"Mike, did you see the bay?"

"It looks like we could walk to the Bahamas. I told you we would have good weather, didn't I?"

"You sure did! What can I do?"

"Get the rest of the groceries. I need to install this new marine radio; Jill got me for my birthday."

Mike walks below and begins to remove the old radio. After a few minutes, Eric walks in.

"Need any help, bud?"

"No, but I had to rip out the old screws—they were too rusty to remove."

"You got new ones?"

"I can only find one in the box. See if you can find the other one in there for me."

"No, Mike, it's empty. Do you have any more screws in the tool box?"

"No. We can put one in for now and pick one up at that little hardware store in the Bahamas."

"You think we'll be alright till then, Mike?"

"Yeah, we can be there before nighttime and pick one up in the morning."

"You're the captain!"

"I'll contact the Coast Guard to make sure our radio is working properly. Alright, mate, let's cast off!"

And, with that, they're on their way.

"We'll motor out of the bay, and then we'll set the sails."

"Aye-aye, Captain Crunch."

Upon reaching blue water, Mike shuts down the diesel, and they begin to set the sails.

"Mike, did you know this cleat and pulley are loose?"

"No! Which one?"

"The one that holds the main sail pulley."

"Damn it! I told Bill to replace that for me. I have a new one here, all he needed were to get was two new bolts to hold it in place. He swore if he could take his girlfriend out for the weekend, he would."

"And you believed him? Well, guess what, he didn't. Do you think this might become a problem for us?"

"Better move it to that other cleat."

"That one looks kind of small, Mike!"

"If it breaks, we can go back to the loose one, but I think we'll be good."

"Mike, are you sure this will work?"

"It's either that or we go back and fight morning traffic to reach Home Depot. You call it, Eric!"

For a split second Eric thinks of all the problems he is leaving behind. He looks ahead at the calm waters and clear blue sky and then back at Mike.

"You're the sailor. If you think we're good, then we're good."

"Look Eric, dolphin to our port. That's a good sign."

"Good! Just, next time Mike, tell me left or right side!"

The wind catches the sail and they are on their way. With a strong steady wind behind them and smooth seas, before long the land and all Eric's problem are behind, ahead the Bahamas and all new adventures.

"Land ho! Look, Eric, the Bahamas!"

"Mikey, you want to get close to anchor for the night?"

"No, this will do. Maybe we can drum up some fish for dinner."

"I'll get the anchor. Tell me when to drop her overboard."

Eric looks over the side, he can see through the clear water as if he were looking into a giant fish bowl.

"Mike, look at the colors on those reefs."

"Have you ever gone diving in the Bahamas before, Eric?"

"No, but I can't wait to jump in."

"Can we use a spear gun here?"

"No, not this close, but if we go back out some we can. It's getting late, so let's fish off the boat today. We can dive tomorrow."

"Cool, do we have cell coverage here, Mike?"

"No, there is only one Cell Company out here, and it's not our carrier."

Eric, "I can't wait to call Barbie and tell her about that sailfish we hooked on. It must have weighed at least eighty pounds."

"I think it was more like sixty Eric." "I just wish we had it on film when it came out of the water tailing like it did—three times in a row."

"I wish I could have landed it."

"It is almost impossible to land a fish that size from a sailboat. You have to be able to follow it and back up at times."

"You did good to keep it on as long as you did Eric."

"I have a sand patch marked on my GPS and its coming up. Get ready to drop anchor."

As he looks down, Eric sees a group of reef jack as they dart across the bottom. Their colors shimmer like neon lights.

"Okay, now, Eric, let her go."

With a splash, the anchor begins its descent into their domain, drifting silently, deeper and deeper into the clear green sea. As it lands on the ocean floor, it causes a small cloud of sand to rise and then gently settle back; covering most of the anchor's four-foot chain. Suddenly, as if on cue, the jacks explode in unison. As the sun's rays bounce off their bodies, they look like an underwater rainbow, dashing from one coral head to another, as they disappear into the distance.

"Wow, Mike, did you see those jacks?"

"No."

"Where are the fishing rods, Mike?"

"They're downstairs under the bunk, to your left. The artificial baits are there too."

"Got them! Let's do this."

They fish for a while and after dinner of fresh snapper they turn in early, and eagerly await tomorrow.

"Wake up, sleepyhead," says Mike the next morning.

"You know, Barbie brings me coffee in bed in the morning."

"And Maxx licks your feet, so get over it. Let's go! We have things to do, and you want to make that call, right?"

"I sure do. Let's go."

They untie the small dingy from the bow and set it overboard.

"You know how to row this thing, right, Eric?"

"Oh, I have to row?"

"Well, who is the captain here, you or me?"

"Yeah, okay, I'll row."

"Are you going to stand in the front with a sword in your hand, Captain Crunch?"

"All I have is a butter knife. You think that will work?"

"I'm sure it will. Now, let's go, Mike."

Once they get to shore, Eric is able to make his phone call.

"Hi, Barbie."

"Eric, where are you calling from?"

"Our cells don't work here, so I had to use a payphone."

"How is the trip? Are you guys having fun?"

"Great, babe. I hooked a sailfish!"

"You did? Did you bring him in?"

"*Land* him, baby. The correct term—*land* him."

"What ever, did you get him then?"

"No, if we had been on a motorboat, I would have had a much better chance. But in a sailboat it's very difficult to land a fish that size. I did catch a six-pound yellowtail last night and an eight-pound grouper. We're going to cook them when Javy gets here."

"About that, Eric, he called to tell me that the city inspector failed the job he is doing at the Davie Auditorium. He won't be able to fly out tomorrow."

"What!"

"He will fly out on Saturday."

"Oh, man, I'll have to tell Mike. We wanted to sail out before that storm got any closer."

"Eric, promise me you won't sail out if it intensifies."

"We won't. What is the weather station saying about it now?"

"It has stalled, and the computers are not sure what it might do next."

"Great, we'll be stuck here for days!"

"Yeah, mon, you might."

"We are in the Bahamas, Barbie, not Jamaica, mon."

"Got to go now, babe. Love you."

"So, what time will Javy arrive now?"

"Oh, yeah, the only flight he could get was a four P.M. flight."

"Great, that means we'll have to wait till Sunday to leave."

"Looks that way, babe."

"Let me go tell Mike, I'll call you as soon as I can, love you Barbie!"

"Me, too mon, Bye!"

Eric laughs at her little joke and hangs up.

He proceeds across the small town's plaza, and passes two old men playing cards under a huge, shady tree. He looks at their bare feet and notices that even though they seem very poor, they appear happy and content with their existence. One of the old men looks up from his game.

"Good morning, young man."

"Good morning, gentlemen."

He crosses the gravel road and approaches the small hardware store at the other end of the plaza, with its brightly painted red-and-yellow sign. He steps inside and notices a tall, muscular black man with a torn apron and ripped shorts.

"May I help you, sir?"

"Yes, I'm looking for my friend."

"Over here, Eric!"

"Mikey, I have good news and bad news."

"Is the good news that you found two rich and beautiful ladies looking for a romantic evening?"

The tall man lets out a loud laugh, startling Eric who has now passed him and has his back to him.

"No, not quite."

"Then give me the bad news first."

"Javy can't fly in till Saturday."

"Great! What is the good news then?"

"The storm is stalled for now."

"Well, I got the bolts for the cleat and the screws for the radio."

"Let's pay and get back to the boat. I'm starved Eric."

"Yea Me too, all that rowing made me hungry."

They pay the store clerk. Eric puts the two bolts for the cleat in his pocket, and Mike takes the two screws for the radio and puts them in his pants pocket.

Back on the boat, Mike wants to get right to work.

"Eric, you want to start changing the bolts on that cleat while I cook?"

"Sure, where are your tools?"

"Lift up the seat cushion closest to the ladder, and you'll find what you need."

"Got it!"

Eric removes the cushion and digs out the old box. *Let's see what we have here,* he says to himself. Assessing what he will need for the job, he digs into the plastic box and begins to retrieve a rusty adjustable wrench from the top plastic tray and a flat-blade screwdriver from the bottom of the box. He goes back on deck.

"Mike, have you got any WD-40?"

"It should be in the same compartment!"

"Can you throw it up here, so I don't have to go back down Mike?"

"Hold on a minute, and I'll pitch it your way."

A few seconds later, he throws it up to Eric.

"Here you go, Eric."

"Did you give the food a shot of WD-40 for flavoring, Mike?"

"Hey, you can call my wife fat and my kids ugly, but don't mess with my cooking!"

"Cooking? Is that what they're calling it now?"

"You want to cook,. Eric ?"

"No, thanks."

"Mike, I'm going to need your help to get one of the bolts out."

"Now?"

"Yeah, if you can."

"I'll be there in a second."

"Take your time."

After a ten-minute fight with the rusty bolt, the old bolts are out and the new bolts are in place. The cleat and pulley are now firmly in place.

"Good job, Eric!"

"All in a day's work for a first mate."

"Man, whatever you're cooking sure smells good!"

"I need to get back and turn it down."

"I'll go with you."

"It is amazing what little WD- 40 will do to food." Mike says with a smile.

They turn and head down the stairs to the galley, not realizing, that, in their haste, they fail to move the rope from the smaller, weaker pulley to the newer, stronger one they have just installed.

After dinner, Eric and Mike take off their shirts and dive into the water for a swim. Mike does not realize he has not taken the screws from his pants. As they swim back and forth from the beautiful coral bottom to the boat, the tiny screws fall out of Mike's loose-fitting pants.

The next afternoon, Mike and Eric sit under a coconut tree on the sandy beach, looking out over the slow-breaking waves.

Mike, "I see it coming low, at four o'clock."

"I see it too!"

The seaplane begins to descend, looking like a giant pelican, its white belly skipping smoothly along the gentle waves. The pilot now gives more power to the right engine and the plane turns in their direction. With a burst from its mighty engines, the plane makes its way up the ramp. Mike and Eric get up and brush the powder-like sand from their shorts. The plane has now taxied past them to its final destination. The engines turning slower and slower, finally they come to a full stop. The small door opens and the first passenger out is Javy.

"How was your flight?" Eric asks.

"Good! You guys, I can't believe how clear the water looks from up there."

"Yea we know! Welcome aboard, Javy!"

"Thanks Mike. Are we sailing out tonight?"

"I think it would be best to get an early start in the morning. What's the latest on the storm Javy?"

"Last I heard, it was moving again, but very slowly. The weather station mentioned something about a trough that will have some kind of effect on it."

"What kind of effect?" Eric asks.

"I was on the phone and wasn't paying all that much attention."

"I'll check the weather radio before we sail," Mike says.

The next morning, Mike wakes up at six o'clock.

"Rise and shine men. You too, Javy!" Mike says.

Eric steps outside to a beautiful day. The sun's rays penetrate the deep green sea, making a spectrum of colors unlike anything he has ever seen before.

"Is this not the most beautiful water in the world, or what?" Mike tells them.

Mike is so taken by the beauty of the day that he forgets to check on the storm.

"You boys ready to sail?' Mike asks them.

"Sure! Get ready to weigh anchor!"

Eric says, "That's captain talk for you to get the anchor up. Call him Captain Crunch—he likes that!"

"Okay! And what do I call you Eric?"Javy asks with a smirk.

"You can call me anything you want, just don't call me late for lunch!"

"Mike, are you going to set the sail now?"

"No, Javy, let's motor out some and then we can set the main sail."

They turn the boat around and back out to sea. As they slowly pass the small group of old fishing boats tied to an old milk jug, Javy turns to Eric.

"How would you like to make a living fishing from one of those leaky buckets?"

"Javy, the guys who own those boats are the lucky ones. The rest have to fish from the rocks and piers."

"Man, I won't complain about working overtime again!" Javy states as he shakes his head.

As the sea turns from emerald green to a deep blue, Mike shouts out, "Okay, me buckles, man the sails!"

Eric turns to Javy. "It looks like someone has seen Pirate of the Caribbean once too many times."

They set the main sail, and the ship comes to life. With the wind at her back, she begins to cut her way across the waves. The salt spray showers over the bow and creates mini-rainbows that disappear behind the stern. Just as fast as they form, Mike shouts out, "Hey, you boys, see this heading on the compass? If something happens to me, turn it completely 180 degrees and you will wind up right where we started!"

"Back to the Bahamas or Miami?"

"Back to Miami! Javy, come here so you can take a turn at the wheel."

"Sure thing, Cap!"

That evening after dinner, Eric calls down to the galley.

"Mike, come up here a minute."

"What's up?"

"Look at those waves. They seem to be getting bigger."

"The weather station is forecasting strong squalls for tonight. Should we turn back?"

Mike, "No, keep her heading into the wind. It will take us off course a little, but I think this is our best bet."

It is now eight P.M. The waves have grown in size from two to four to six to ten feet. They are now tossing the small ship from side to side in what has become a fight for survival. Mike is at the wheel. A flash of lighting lights up the night and he is horrified to see the small cleat and pulley are still holding the main sail. Knowing it's only a matter of time before it gives out in this turmoil, he yells down to Eric and Javy.

"Eric, we forgot to run the sail through the larger pulley we replaced. We need to change over, before this one breaks and we lose the sail."

"How can we change the rigging in this mess Mike?"

"We can't!"

"So what do we do?"

"I have a spare rope in the anchor compartment. We need to get it and run it through the new pulley. Tie it next to the one on the main sail. This will give us two anchor points for the sail. You guys put on your life vests and bring me one too."

Eric and Javy strap on their vests and hand Mike his.

"I'm going for the rope," Eric says.

"Okay, Eric," Mike says, "but tie yourself to the bow railing with the dock rope first."

Tying one end of the rope around his waist, Eric maneuvers past Mike and leans over while Javy holds Eric's belt with one hand and the ladder's railing with the other.

"Okay, let go," Eric says. "I'm tied off."

Slowly Eric crawls to the anchor compartment, he leans over and reaches into the compartment, his fingers fumbling in the darkness.

Mike says, "It should be under the anchor rope."

A large wave breaks over the bow, making him temporarily lose his grip and slip onto his side. Frantically, Eric grabs for the side of the open hatch and holds on with both hands.

Javy yells, "Are you okay, Eric?"

Wiping the salt from his eyes and mouth, Eric says, "I'm good! I've got it now!"

With the rope firmly in his left hand, he crawls to the other side of the boat, just out of sight of Mike and Javy.

"Javy, the rope is too short. Untie me and I will tie off on the other side."

"No, it's too dangerous."

"We don't have a choice—now undo me."

Mike says, "Do it, Jav."

Javy leans over and unties the rope.

"It's loose. Pull it!"

Holding onto the railing with his right hand, he pulls the now-slack rope, bringing it closer and closer with his free hand. Finally, he clinches the soggy rope's end in his left hand. He throws the loose end over the railing and quickly ties it off using both hands to work the rope as fast as he can.

"I'm tied off!"

"Good. Be careful." Javy shouts back.

Taking one end of the rope, Eric threads it through the new pulley. Not realizing he has a knot only four feet from the end, he ties it to the sail.

"I got it through. I'm going to throw it your way, Mike, so be ready."

Mike shouts back, "Let her rip."

Eric throws it.

"Got it! Come back so Javy can hold the wheel and you can help me tie it off."

Eric now must make the arduous trek back to safety.

"I'll untie myself and throw this one too so you can pull me in, okay?"

"Do it, we're ready," Javy shouts back.

Taking a deep breath, Eric unties the rope from the boat railing and turns to head back to safety. But before he has a chance to throw his rope, he runs his other hand along the new rope that will now hold the mast and he feels the knot he missed in the darkness. His stomach tenses up. Should he pull back the rope from Mike and untie the knot, or do they take a chance on it not making a difference? Before he is able to call out to Mike for advice, a change in the wind forces the mast to shift violently from one side to the other, putting a tremendous strain on the now-stressed cleat.

Suddenly, Eric hears a loud popping noise behind him. Before he has a chance to react, the cleat breaks and the mast is now hurtling toward him. It catches him off balance and strikes the back of his head with so much force, it throws him overboard.

Mike is thrown off balance by the same violent gust. As he regains his footing, he is horrified to see Eric's body hit the railing and tumble into the churning sea.

"Javy, get up here now!"

"What happened?"

"Quick, take the wheel." He ties off the new mast rope.

"What happened? Where's Eric?"

"He fell overboard!"

"Pull him back in Mike!" "I can't he was not tied off!"

"What! Turn around, Mike."

"We can't! We'll capsize if we turn."

Mike pulls out the searchlight from under the hatch and plugs it in. He turns on the light and peers into the darkness. While holding on with one hand, he swings the light with his other hand to scan it over the foreboding, churning black sea, hoping against hope to catch a glimpse of Eric. While Mike works the light, Javy frantically shouts Eric's name at the top of his lungs.

"Javy, Get my hand-held GPS. It's on my bunk. Write down our position and call the Coast Guard. Tell them what has happened and where we're at."

Javy stands on the top run of the ladder and begins his search. As the beam from his flashlight shines across the floor, he is horrified to see the marine radio in about a half inch of seawater. His knees weaken at the sight. The one screw did not hold the radio in place. Picking it up, he sees the wires have been ripped from inside.

"Mike, the radio has broken loose and it's useless."

Mike grabs for his empty pants pocket now, remembering the screws he forgot to replace.

The small boat has taken in several inches of water through the open hatch, its two bilge pumps franticly work to keep the small craft from going under.

Javy makes his way down the steps and into the cabin, he shines his flash light from one side to the other until he finds the GPS floating in the water next to a spare life preserver; he picks it up and grabs a towel from the bathroom, in an effort to drys off the unit as best he can. He fumbles with the front knobs and is both relived and delighted when the unit light comes on.

"Can you get a GPS reading Javy?"

"No!" Not yet!"

"Bring it up here on deck. Any better?"

"No, it's too damn cloudy. The satellite signals won't come in."

They spend the rest of the night scanning the waves and hopelessly calling Eric's name into the darkness.

The next morning, the sky is cloudy, but thankfully the seas have calmed to large swells. It has been a long and sleepless night for Mike and Javy. Their eyes are bloodshot from the lack of sleep and constant salt spray. Their voices hoarse from a night of shouting back and forth constantly calling out Eric's name in the dark, hoping against hope he would answers back.

Taking advantage of the lull in the seas, they are able to reposition the mast-rigging rope and take the knot out of the new rope.

"What do we do now, Mike?"

"Our best bet is to head back."

"Back to the Bahamas or to Miami?"

"Javy, judging from the GPS positioning, it will be about the same time to the Bahamas as to Key West."

"So, it's Key West, right, Mike?"

"How long do you think it will take us to get there Mike?'

"No telling, if the winds helps we could be in Key West in about eighteen to twenty hours."

"Yeah, let's hope the wind picks up some."

"Mike, do you think we can we repair the radio?"

"No, the water got inside the works."

"I just wish we could tell someone right now.'

"Me To, Javy."

"He had his vest on. Let's pray he's still alive."

"Damn it! Oh, man ... Barbie! What do we tell her, Mike?"

"The truth that is all we can tell her, and pray he is alive."

Chapter Four
The Rescue

Meantime, the luxury ship *Christina Milan* is making her way through the Gulf of Mexico back to her home base in Costa Rica. Onboard is the boat's namesake, the beautiful twenty-two-year-old daughter of Emilio Milan, a self-made millionaire. She is returning home from a visit with her mother in Coral Gables, Florida. With her long black hair and deep green eyes, she is a stunning beauty. She has her mother's good looks and her father's tenacity and temper. Unfortunately, she did not inherit his kind heart or his morals.

In her suite, Christina brushes her hair. There is a knock at the door.

"Come in!"

"Good morning, Senorita Christina."

"Good morning, Alva."

"Can I bring you breakfast in your quarters?"

"No, I think I'll have it on deck. It's too pretty of a morning to stay inside."

"As you wish, Senorita."

Alva leaves. As Christina steps out on deck, she feels the sun's warm rays on her face. She sees Enrique sitting on a lounge chair by the back railing, writing on a yellow pad.

"Are you writing your boyfriend, Enrique?" She teases.

"No!" Enrique snaps back.

She walks on by, opens the door, and steps inside the captain's office. Alva stays outside on the deck with Enrique.

Alva says, "Enrique, you held your tongue!"

"I almost said, 'At least I have a man in my life.'"

"Be kind, Enrique. You know how devastated she is over finding Armando with that girl at the discotheque."

"With her money, she'll have a bunch of men waiting in line when we get back Alva."

"That's the problem—all they want is her money."

"Oh, poor little rich girl!"

"Don't talk like that, Enrique. Her father has been good to you. He took you in off the streets, gave you a job and a home. You and Christina practically grew up together."

"She looks at me as if I'm just the help."

Alva interrupts, "Enrique, you *are* the help."

"Whatever!" he says, looking up from his pad.

Suddenly, he jumps up.

"Alva, did you just see that?"

"See what?"

"Look over there, the orange thing floating out there."

"I don't see anything!"

"Wait, Alva, look straight out to your left. It will pop up again. Look, look right there!"

"I see it! I see it now, Enrique!"

"I think it's a person, Alva. Quick, call the captain. I'll keep my eyes on it. Hurry! Hurry!"

Alva runs inside the captain's office.

"Quick, Captain Hernandez, come outside! There's a body floating!"

The captain grabs his binoculars and runs after Alva. Enrique is standing on the bottom of the ships railing leaning out over the top one. Look there captain, it just went down, here it comes up again...

Raising the binoculars, the captain shouts back to the first mate.

"Reduce speed, Pedro, and bring her around port side. Man the skiff."

Enrique go with Pedro and helps him.

"Yes, sir."

Christina, having heard all the commotion, is now outside with them.

"Is that a person, Captain?" she asks.

"Yes, it is."

"Are they alive?"

"Can't tell from here, Senorita."

"Hurry up, Enrique!" Alva says.

"If it's a man, he better be good looking," Enrique remarks.

"Captain, do you think it's safe to bring him on board?" Christina asks.

"We are bound by maritime law to render assistance. If that person is alive, we can save him or her. If they are dead, we can bring them back to their family."

"I hope they're alive. I don't want to bring a dead body onto Daddy's new boat."

"I'm sure your father will not object either way, Senorita."

Pedro and Enrique push the small skiff off and its engine comes alive. The little boat skips along the waves closing the distance in a short time. Pedro brings the boat alongside and puts the motor in neutral. They carefully coast alongside the lifeless body.

They untie the loose rope from around his waist, and pull the unconscious young man onboard. Pedro throws the boat in gear, and the little engine screams as they make their way back to the now-stopped ship.

"Is he alive, Captain?" Christina asks.

"Yes, but he has a nasty bump on the back of the head."

Seeing the handsome young man on the deck, she gasps and turns to Alva.

"Oh, my God, Alva. My dream! Could this be the man in my dream?"

Caught by surprise Alva asks. "What man?"

"The dream I told you about. Remember? When I was seventeen, I dreamed I was sitting on the beach and a young man arrived on a small fishing boat. He got out and walked over to me. He took me by the hand, kissed me softly, and took me back to this beautiful place."

Alva looks at Enrique, not knowing what to say.

"Maybe it is him, Senorita," she finally replies.

The captain steps in.

"Pedro, did you hear any Maydays or Coast Guard calls last night?"

"No, sir."

"I'll contact the Coast Guard and ask if they have any missing boats in this area."

"Captain, wait!"

"Senorita, I must call the proper authorities."

"I will have my father call them."

"You don't understand. I can lose my license."

"Captain, what is more important—a license or a ship to command it with? I will call my father now, and he will handle this whole affair. Now, there will be no more talk of this."

The captain lowers his head and walks away.

Enrique reaches into the unconscious man's pants pocket.

"He has a wallet."

"Give it to me," Christina says.

"Yes, Senorita."

She takes the soggy wallet and heads to her quarters. She walks in, closes the door, and locks it. She picks up the ship-to-shore.

"Hi, Father."

"Hi, Chrissie. How was your stay with your mother?"

"Good, Dad. She's on a new healthy-diet kick."

"Sounds like your mommy! And your stepdad?"

"He was away on business. Dad, you're not going to believe what just happened."

"Please, no surprises. I'm not as young as I used to be, and the ship is not paid for yet."

"No, Dad, we just saved someone from the sea."

"Refugees from Cuba?"

"No, Dad, a young man"—she looks at his driver's license—"an American, I think."

"Did the captain call the proper authorities?"

"Yes, Daddy, it's all taken care of. There is someone knocking at my door. I have to go. I'll call you later."

"Bye, baby."

"Bye, Dad."

She hangs up and attends to the door.

"Who is it?"

"It's me, Enrique."

"Yes, come in."

"The Captain wants to know what your dad had to say. Do we return to Miami with him or do we continue to Costa Rica?"

"We continue to Costa Rica."

"But, he looks American. Your dad does not want us to return him to Miami?"

Enrique looks at the wallet in her hand.

"I thought I made it clear that we are going home, to Costa Rica."

"Yes, Senorita, I will tell the captain immediately."

Enrique leaves her quarters and she immediately begins to pull apart the waterlogged wallet. She sees from the driver's license that the man's name is Eric Montana. There is a photo of him with someone who appears to be his girlfriend. She also sees a fire department badge and another photo, this one of the unconscious man with a young man and a dog. All of a sudden, she hears a knock at the door. She quickly shoves the wallet under her bed.

"Come in!"

Alva enters the cabin.

"Can I get you anything to eat, Senorita?"

"No, Alva, I'll get something later."

"Senorita, was there any information on the young man in his wallet?"

"No, there were only papers, and they were too soggy to be of any use."

Alva turns to leave.

"Oh, by the way, Alva, do not mention this wallet to anyone. We do not want to him to think we stole anything from him, do we, Alva?"

"As you say, Senorita."

After Alva leaves, Christina takes the wallet and carefully hides it with her belongings.

Meantime, the still-unconscious man has been taken to a spare bunk below. Christina walks down to his room.

"Enrique, has he come to?"

"No, but he did mumble something."

"What?"

"I don't know I could not make what he was saying."

"You stay with him, and if he comes too, get me. I don't care what time it is. Do you understand me, Enrique?"

"Yes, yes, yes, I understand you, loud and clear."

"Good!"

Back on Mike's boat, Javy is at the wheel while Mike tries to gets some rest. Javy spots a large container ship headed their way.

"Mike. Mikey, get up here!"

Mike runs up, his eyes bloodshot from the lack of sleep.

"What's wrong?"

"Look, a ship. We can get alongside and have them called the Coast Guard for us."

"Head that way, so I can see their flag."

Javy steers the boat toward the big orange and blue cargo ship headed straight for them. As they close the distance, the cargo ship begins to let out loud blasts from its steam horns.

"Forget it, Javy."

"What do you mean forget it?"

"Look at the flag—they are Japanese.

What? They won't stop to help?"

"It's not that, it would take them half a mile to stop and how do we communicate with them?"

Besides, we lost the dingy in the storm. If we get too close to them we could be crushed?"

"Get back on course. It's our best bet."

As they pass the big ship, they both look intensely to see if Eric is on the deck.

After twelve more long hours they arrive at Key West. They tie off and run to the duty officer.

"Help us, please! Our friend is still out at sea. He fell overboard yesterday!"

"Calm down, one at a time!"

As they are speaking to the coastguardsman, he picks up the phone and calls the commander. A tall man with a big red mustache walks into the room.

"I'm Commander Tom Anderson. Please explain to me what happened."

"We were hit by a huge squall, and our friend was swept overboard."

"When and where did this happen?"

"Eighteen hours ago, we were headed to Costa Rica, from the Bahamas. We couldn't get a fix on the GPS until six hours later."

The commander turns to Lieutenant Ramos.

"Notify the helicopter crew, and have Commander Abraham of the Diamondback prepare to sail at once!   You men come down with me to the maps room. Maybe we can figure out where you lost him and start the search there."

"Sir, is there a phone I can use to contact our families?" Javy asks.

"Yes, use my office. Follow me."

Javy walks into the captain's office and sits down, not knowing what he will say. He dials Barbie's number. The phone rings. She answers on the third ring.

"Hello, Barbie?"

"Yes!"

"Is that you, Barbie?"

"Of course it's me, Javy, is something wrong? Where is Eric? Why are you calling me instead of him?" She asks in a trembling voice.

"Barbie there was an accident."

"No! No! Javy, he has to be alright!"

"Barbie, he probably is, but he fell overboard."

"Overboard! Where! When, Javy?"

"The Coast Guard is looking for him right now."

"I'm coming! Where are you now, Javy?"

"No, Barbie, stay where you are. They are doing everything possible, and it's better if you stay where you are. If he calls you, you'll be there."

"Javy, when did he fall in?"

"Sunday night."

"And you are calling me now? Why have you taken so long to call, Javy?"

"We had trouble with the radio. You know Eric is tough and he's a survivor."

"Javy, how could you and Mike let this happen to him?"

"There was nothing anyone could have done to prevent it! Maybe it's best if you stay at your mother's. I'm sure if he calls, he'll call your cell."

"Not *if,* Javy. He will call! I know it, I can feel it!"

"You're right, Barbie, he will. I have to go. As soon as I hear something, I'll call you."

The Coast Guard sends out an emergency alarm to all vessels in the vicinity. The local TV stations are contacted. An all-out search for Eric is on.

Unfortunately for Eric, the *Christina Milan* has docked, and her radios are silent. Her crew is now on dry land. There is no one to hear the Coast Guard messages.

Upon their arrival to port, an ambulance was already waiting for them.

"Alva, I'm going to ride with them to the hospital. After Enrique drops you off have him go to the hospital to get me. Tell my dad I'll be home in a bit."

At the hospital admittance office a nurse asks what happened.

Christina says, "We found him floating in the Gulf."

"Were the proper authorities notified?"

"Yes!"

"You are not related to him then?"

"No!"

"Do you know if he has any insurance?"

"No, but my father will take care of the bill."

"And your father's name is?"

"Emilio Milan."

"You're Emilio Milan's daughter?"

"Yes."

"Can I see some form of identification, please?"

Christina opens her purse and dumps out several credit cards with her name, along with several hundred dollars and her gold Rolex.

The nurse looks over her shoulder at the older lady at the other end of the long desk who had been listening to the entire conversation; she walks over picks up Christina's driver's license and then gives a nod of approval to the nurse.

"I'll begin the paperwork," the nurse says.

Just then, the emergency room doctor comes out and addresses Christina.

"I am doctor Morales, I will be treating him."

"Pleased to meet you doctor, I am Christina Milan."

"Are you related?" he asks.

"No."

"Does he have any family here, Miss Milan?"

"No! Is he going to be alright, Doctor?"

"I sent him upstairs for a CAT scan. He received a severe blow to the back of the head."

Someone yells, "Dr. Morales, the young man has come to."

"Excuse me, Miss Milan!"

"Can I see him now, Doctor, she shouts as he leaves?"

"Not just yet. I'll come talk to you as soon as I have examined him. You can wait in the patient's lounge."

Her cell phone rings.

"Hi, Daddy."

"Christina, Alva tells me you are at the hospital with the young man, is this true?"

"Before you start, Dad, I saved his life. I can't just walk away now."

Enrique, who has been with her all morning, scoffs at hearing her comment. He turns to an old woman sitting next to him at the lounge.

"I'm the one that saved his life, not her."

The old woman just smiles and goes back to praying over her rosary.

Emilio says, "He could be wanted by the law for all we know. You should walk away—you have done enough for him already."

"I'm sure he's not wanted by the law."

Enrique says, "Tell him about the wallet."

She covers the phone speaker. "Shut up!"

Just then, the doctor walks in.

"I have to go, Daddy. Bye!"

"I examined him and he seems to have all his faculties and motor skills, but he has no memory of what happened or who he is."

"How long will that last, Doctor?"

"No telling, it could last days, months, or the rest of his life. There's just no telling."

"Can I see him now, Doctor?"

"Yes, but I gave him a sedative. He has a mild concussion and a headache, so don't stay long."

"Okay, thank you, Doctor."

She walks into Eric's room. Enrique waits until she is in, and then follows her in.

"Hi! How do you feel?"

"I feel like my head is two sizes too big."

"My name is Christina Milan."

"You have me at a disadvantage—I can't remember my name. I don't even know how I got here."

Enrique jumps in. "We found you in the ocean."

"Well, thank you. Thank you, both."

"You're welcome. I'm Enrique."

"Enrique, wait for me at the car," Christina says without looking at him.

"Yes, Senorita."

"I saw your orange flotation vest and notified the captain. My father owns the ship that picked you up."

"I don't know how to thank you all. Is anyone looking for me or do you know how I got where you found me?"

"The proper authorities have been notified, but no word as of yet. The doctor wants you to stay for a few days. I will be back tomorrow to see you."

"I don't know how I'm going to pay the bill here."

"Don't worry about that. It's taken care of."

"I must have a guardian angel watching over me."

"Yes, and she has black hair." She smiles and walks out of his room.

Down at the car Christina tells Enrique, "You forget that wallet and mind your place."

"What, I am not allowed to speak now?"

"You need to watch what you say and to whom you say it, about this incident. Now, let's go. One more thing, I'm not that little girl anymore, and you need to respect me."

Enrique does not say a word. He opens the door for her and then jumps into the driver's side.

When Christina and Enrique pull into the circular drive at the Milan estate, Emilio is standing outside talking to the gardener. He looks up to see his daughter.

"Hi, there, little girl."

"Daddy, I'm not a little girl anymore!"

"Sure you are, you will always be—right, Enrique!"

Enrique walks by them both without saying a word.

As Emilio kisses her on the cheek, he asks, "Is something wrong with Enrique?"

"Dad, sometimes he forgets his place. He acts like he is one of us."

"Christina, do you remember when I brought him home? He was only a few years older than you at the time."

"I do, Dad."

"I had my office in San Jose, and I would see him on the street begging for money. He would sleep behind my office in a cardboard box. I would look at him and see myself at his age. I would think about how lucky I was that old man Fuentes saw me working on the docks, took me in, and gave me the opportunity to run his warehouse. The rest is history."

"But, Daddy, he's not anything like you."

"I know, but even though we are all different, we are still all God's children. To me, he is more that just help."

"Daddy, you know I treat him more like a brother than an employee."

"Good, that's what I like to hear. Now, tell me about your trip and this young man you rescued. If I recall my fairy-tale stories correctly, the knight is supposed to save the princess, not the princess saves the knight. Come, let's go inside and you can tell me all about your rescue at sea."

The next day, Christina arrives at the hospital. She goes to Eric's room, only to find it empty. She then makes her way to the nurse's station.

"Where is the patient who was in room 8?"

"Oh, he is feeling much better. I think he is in the garden with one of the nurse assistants."

Christina walks out to the garden and sees Eric sitting by a water fountain, looking at the fish. Just then, a pretty young woman in a nurse's outfit passes by her with a lunch tray in her hand. Christine grabs her arm.

"Is that for him?"

"Yes, it is."

"I'll take it to him."

The young woman steps back, but Christina grabs the tray.

"I'm his fiancée." The young woman reluctantly releases the tray.

"Well, you're looking much better today!" Christina says to Eric as she hands him the tray.

"Oh, thank you, Christina!"

"Yes, at least your memory is improving."

"I guess so. You know, I can't begin to thank you for all you have done for me. You mentioned that you are the one that spotted me floating?"

"Why, yes, I did, but let's not talk of that now."

"How will I ever repay you for that?"

"Get better and maybe you can take me out to dinner."

He smiles back at her. "It would be my pleasure, but I don't have any money. I don't even have a place to stay."

"Don't let that worry you. When they release you, you may stay with us."

"Oh, I can't do that. You have done more than enough for me already."

"Nonsense! We have a big place, and you can stay until we find out who you are. Has the doctor said when you can leave?"

"No, not yet."

"Let me talk to him. In the meantime, you eat your lunch."

"Thanks again."

"Don't mention it. I'll be right back."

She walks in and sees the doctor standing by the nurse's station.

"May I speak with you, Doctor?"

"Yes, Miss Milan."

"It's about the young man in room 8."

"What do you need to know, Miss?"

"Is there anything we can do to help bring back his memory, Doctor?"

"Call him by his name if you know it. Maybe you can take him to places that are familiar to him. Do you know his name?"

She thinks for a second. "No, I don't. When can he go home?"

"Well, I would like to keep him for another twenty-four hours."

She sees the young assistant nurse standing a few feet away and listening intensely.

"I would like him to go home with me today."

"For his own good, I feel he should remain under my care for at least twenty-four more hours."

"Doctor, our family physician will call you. He can take care of him at our home. Please make all the necessary arrangements to release him now."

"If you wish, but I must protest your haste to remove him."

"Fine, Doctor, I'll take full responsibility."

She returns to find Eric sitting on the edge of the fountain, eating his lunch.

"Good news! The doctor said you can leave with me."

"What about the hospital bill?"

"Don't worry about that."

"I insist you must let me pay you back, Christina."

"Sure, will that be cash or credit?" They both laugh.

They walk down to the car where Enrique is waiting.

"Enrique, right?" Eric asks.

"Yes, sir, you remembered my name."

"Yeah, now if I could only remember mine."

Enrique remembers seeing the wallet. "But didn't you—?"

Christina stops him and with a stern look, she snaps. "Enrique, let's go, my father is waiting."

They get in the car and drive away to the Milan estate.

As they make their way through the town and out into the lush countryside, Eric is captivated by the beautiful flowers and the old-style rock fences used to separate the properties. As they begin their ascent up the long winding road that leads to the Milan estate, he can now look down at the sea, with its waves gently rolling over the large rocks.

The landscape is dotted with large green palm trees that seem to climb endlessly up the sides of the hills.

Christina asks, "What do you think of our country so far?"

"It is breathtaking, to say the least. I have never seen the sea on one side of a road and lush green pasture on the other."

"That's Costa Rica for you."

"Do you think you have been here before?"

"If I have, I have no recollection of it."

Passing under a large stone archway, they enter a large circular drive with beautiful red and yellow flowers on both sides and a large circular fountain in the middle. Upon arriving at the home, they are met by Alva.

"You look much better than you did when we found you."

"You were there also?" Eric asks.

"Yes, we all were there. As a matter of fact—"

Christina interrupts her. "Later, Alva, my father is waiting."

"Yes, Senorita."

They walk inside.

"Where is my father, Alva?"

"He is in the study."

She takes Eric by the hand.

"Let's go meet Daddy."

They walk down a long corridor. On the wall a large hand-painted oil portrait of a man on a black horse and a large black wooden carving of a horse. At the end of the hall are two large dark-stained oak doors. Christina swings open the doors, and they step into a large room with an extensive collection of books. To the side is a beautiful mahogany wine rack, and in the middle is a large hand-crafted desk. Eric hears a man's voice and sees Emilio Milan standing on a balcony off the room, holding a telephone.

Eric looks at Emilio on the balcony with the ocean at his back, and he can't help, but to wander what would have become of him if not for Christina and him.

He motions them in and gestures to Eric to sit in one of the large velvet-covered seats. Eric sits down and, as he begins to sink into the soft chair, as he observe his new benefactor. He is very well dressed, in his late forties with black hair, and a neatly trimmed beard—not a tall man, but he looks fit, as if he has done manual labor at one time.

"It's a deal then, Juan, I'll be at your office tomorrow and we can finalize the details. You have my word today, and you will have your check by Friday. I am sure the bank will take either." He hangs up and turns to Christina and Eric. "Sorry about that, kids. Business ... you just can't get away from it!"

"You don't try very hard either, Daddy."

He smiles. "No, I don't, do I?"

He firmly shakes Eric's hand. "Emilio Milan."

"It's a pleasure to meet you, sir. I can't express my gratitude to you and your family enough, sir."

He smiles and looks at his daughter. "It's her you need to thank."

"I know. She's the one who saw me floating."

"You did? You didn't tell me that!"

"Daddy, don't embarrass me!"

"Let's celebrate your good fortune and my daughter's good eyes." He opens a bottle of red wine. "Do you like red wine?"

"I don't know, sir."

"Well, I guess we'll just have to find out. Christina, what are we going to call our guest?"

"I don't know, Daddy."

"Do you have any preference, son?"

"Not really, sir."

Emilio looks at the bottle of wine on the mahogany table next to his desk. The label reads Don Antonio Selects 1892.

"How about Antonio?"

"No, Daddy, but Tony sounds good."

"Would you like to be called Tony?"

"Sure, it's better than hey you!" They all laugh.

Eric samples the wine. "Sir, I don't know how much I know about wine, but this is very good."

"Well, I'll tell you this, Tony, we don't know anything about you, but we do know you have good taste in wine."

"I have this wine shipped in from Spain, to my home and to a select few restaurants I frequent. This is a little awkward for me. Usually, this is where I ask the young man my daughter brings home to tell me a little about himself."

"Well, sir, if a little will do, then I can tell you about my last twenty-four hours."

They all have a good laugh.

"Honestly, sir, I have no way to thank you for your hospitality and all you and your daughter have done. Also, the hospital bill."

"What hospital bill?" Emilio asks.

Christina quickly chimes in. "Let's not talk of hospitals or of sea rescues. Let's talk of tomorrow and where we will take you for your first visit to Costa Rica, Tony."

After they talk and drink some more wine, Emilio tells Tony he must speak with his daughter privately for a moment, and asks him to wait for them in the living room.

"Christina I agreed to bring him here with us for a few days, but only a few days' until we find out whom and where he came from and help him get back."

"Of course dad, I would not have it any other way.

"Good, now let get back to our guest."

Chapter Five
Hope Fades

The phone rings. Barbie stares at it solemnly and then picks it up.

"Oh, hi, Karl!"

"'Oh, hi, Karl?' You don't have to sound so disappointed to hear my voice, doll face."

"I'm sorry, Karl, but I was hoping it was Eric, or news about him."

"I'm sure he'll turn up just fine. Any news from the Coast Guard?"

"No, we haven't heard anything yet. Channels 7 and 4 have covered the story, but no one has called."

"We still need to make the trip to L.A Barbie. Will you be up to it?"

"I don't know!"

"Barbie, you have to go on."

"I need time. It's only been a few days, Karl."

"I know, but it's only a few weeks away and you need to get mentally ready. It's not every day a major record company asks you to audition for them, kid."

"I'll be ready. Just ask them to give me a few more days. Life is not the same for me without Eric. I counted on him for everything."

"I know, kid, but I'm still here for you, and you know I will be there with you every step of the way. I'll see if they will push it back a few more days, but remember kid, I am here and we can do this thing together, Barbie."

"Thank you Karl, I have to go. I'll talk to you later. I have another call. Bye." She presses her call-waiting button.

"Hi, Javy."

"Barbie, I just got your message."

"Thanks for calling back, Javy. Would you do me a favor?"

"Sure, name it."

"It's Maxx."

"What's wrong with him?"

"He seems so sad. He's not even doing his growling when he greets me in the morning. Would you take him with you? Maybe the other dogs will help cheer him up?"

"No problem. I'll be more than glad to bring him here until Eric gets back."

She is silent.

"He will come back. He loves you too much not to."

She begins to cry. "I have to go. Bye!"

Later that day, she drives to her parents' home. She steps inside and finds her mother sitting in the kitchen looking out the window.

"Hi, Mom. Good thing I'm not a burglar!"

"I guess my mind is somewhere else."

"I know, Mom, I find myself doing a lot of that." They hug and begin to cry.

"He was so much like a son!"

"No, Mother, he still is. Don't talk of him in the past tense."

"You're right, we need to believe and pray that he will return safely to us."

Just then, her father walks in.

"We all have to keep a positive attitude—now, let's stop this crying. How about I take the two prettiest girls in Miami out to dinner?"

"Sure, Dad, let's wash up and be on our way."

Back at the fire station 6, right after roll call, Smith tells Mike he has a phone call on Line 2. Mike runs to pick it up. It's Javy.

"Hi, Javy, how are you holding up?"

"Mike, I can't shake this feeling that we could have done more."

"Don't do that to yourself, Javy. We did all that we could have, under the circumstances."

"Mike, I have one more week of vacation. I'm thinking of flying to the islands and looking for him. Maybe he washed up on some island and has no money to get back."

"Javy, where would you start?"

"I don't know. That's why I'm calling you. Where should I go?"

"The Coast Guard determined more or less where we were when it happened. There are a lot of small islands nearby, and we can only hope that he was picked up by someone."

"Then why haven't they brought him back or called for someone to come get him?"

"I don't know, Javy, but don't say any of this to Barbie. She needs to keep her faith that he'll come home soon."

"I won't, but I have to do something. I can't just sit around here."

"Javy, do you have any idea how many islands there are out there? He could have drifted to any one of those ten thousand islands. He could be anywhere. Most of those islands are not even inhabited!"

"Yeah, I know, but doing nothing is killing me."

"Hang in there, Javy. He'll turn up, if he made it to one of those islands. Knowing him, he will make a fire to let people know were he is."

"Mike, you know the Coast Guard called the search off today?"

"Yes, I know. For all we know, he is on that Japanese freighter that passed us by and they'll ship him home in a few days."

"I hope so!"

"Javy, I've got to go now—the alarm just went off. Stay in touch."

Back at his home, Javy picks up a worn photo album. He looks at the picture of Eric and him riding their four-wheel-drive ATVs at Lost Lake, both of them covered in mud. He thinks about how this is now a community of upscale homes and wishes he could go back in time to those happy and carefree days. Just then, his cell phone rings and he sees it is Heather.

"How are you doing, Javy?"

"I'm looking at some old photos of Eric and Barbie before I met you."

"Javy, you need to put on a strong face for Barbie and Eric's parents. Have you talked to his father or mom lately?"

"Heather, I can't bring myself to go see them. I feel like I let them and Eric down."

"There was nothing you could have done, Javy. You were not even on deck when it happened."

"Yes, I know, but I can't help but think that if I had been up there with him, things would have turned out differently."

"Differently how, Javy? Maybe we would be looking for you both now."

"I wish they were!"

"Don't say that—or even think it! Eric will be fine, and I'm sure he is glad you're not lost out there too."

"That's easy to say, but it doesn't help me when I wake up at two o'clock in the morning back on that boat, calling out his name and peering into the dark."

"Javy, I know you don't want to hear this, but maybe you should talk to someone about this."

"What? Some kind of shrink, maybe?"

"Honey, please don't get upset, but you have gone through something very traumatic and there is nothing wrong with seeing someone who might be able to help."

"No, just as soon as Eric gets home, this will all end. Until then, I'll be fine. I have to go, Heather. Bye!"

Chapter Six
A New Life in Coasta Rica

As the morning sun penetrate the glass and warms his face, Tony stand by the kitchen window and looks out at the ocean.

"Good morning, Tony, how did you sleep?"

"Very well, Mr. Milan, thank you."

"Tony, after breakfast would you like to accompany me for the day on a drive?"

"Yes, sir, I would like that very much, sir. The doctor told me that a familiar sight might help jog my memory, so I am willing to go anywhere—it just might help."

"I don't know what familiar might be in your case, but I'm sure it won't hurt, either."

Soon Christina joins them at the breakfast table.

"Good morning, Daddy. You too, Tony. How was your night, Tony?"

"Good, thank you, Christina."

Emilio says, "Tony and I are going to drive to Piedra Negara. Would you like to accompany us, Christina?"

"No, you two go. I have some last-minute shopping to do."

"I forget—a woman always has some kind of last-minute shopping to do, right, Tony?"

"I guess so, sir."

"Well, if you must know, Daddy, it's not for me, it's for Tony. He can't go around in Enrique's old clothes."

Enrique, who is pouring their coffee, asks, "Why not? They're Dockers!"

"Alright, you two!" Emilio says.

"Sir, what is a Piedra Negara?"

"First, call me Emilio. That is the name of my favorite ranch."

"Favorite? How many do you have, sir, I mean, Emilio?"

Emilio laughs. "Just a couple."

After breakfast, the three men load a few things into the Land Rover and begin the ride down the hill into town. Again, Tony marvels at the beauty of the sea, with its backdrop of mountains and the shimmering, white sandy beaches.

"This is certainly one of the most beautiful places I have ever seen, sir, I mean, Emilio."

"Our ancestors would tell us as children that the land calls to you and she will never let you leave her."

"Is that why you stay, sir? From what I have seen, you can live anywhere you want."

"True, but I would not have this."

"What about your Christina? Is she as passionate about living here as you?"

"I would like to think so. Her mother lives in a very nice place in Florida, but Christina chose to stay here with me."

"You must be very proud, sir."

"Yes, Tony, I truly am."

Tony notices that Enrique is looking at him as Emilio is talking about Christina, but he does not make any comment.

As the Land Rover heads away from the sea, Emilio turns to Enrique.

"Do you need to stop at the village and see your grandmother?"

"No, thank you. She is visiting with her sister, in San Jose."

They begin the two-hour trip down the bumpy road to the ranch. As they drive, Tony looks at the cattle on both sides of the road.

"Are some of these yours?"

"The cattle on both sides of the road for the last hour are mine."

"Wow! That's a lot of beef! I see you have mostly Brahma cows, and your bulls all seem to be Black Angus."

Enrique's mouth drops. "He's a cowboy."

"You know cattle, Tony?" Emilio asks.

"I'm not sure, but I know I can tell the difference between those two breeds."

"Wonderful, we might find out who you are yet."

"Maybe he is La Rata," offers Enrique.

"La what-ta?"

"La Rata. It means the rat."

"La Rata is a notorious cattle thief. We have been trying to catch him for years."

"No, Enrique, I don't think we have a cattle-rustler as our house guest."

"No, not unless I was going to swim them out of the country." They all laugh.

Finally, they turn down a road with a lock on the front gates. The gates are held by two giant tree trunks, with a third stretched over the top. The words *Piedra Negara* are carved in the middle.

Tony reads the sign out loud. "Piedra Negara. Emilio, why do you call this place the black rock?"

Enrique's mouth drops open again. "Tony, you can speak Spanish too?"

"I understand all that you say. It's just my pronunciation that's not all that good."

"Are you of Latino decent, Tony?" Emilio asks.

"I don't know. I might be, or maybe—"

Enrique jumps in. "Maybe your previous job required you to speak both languages."

"Yeah, maybe, Enrique. If only I could remember what I did for a living."

"In time, Tony. You need to give yourself more time. Anything is possible, and I truly believe this trip might have some positive effect on you yet."

"Let's hope so, sir."

Enrique jumps out and opens the large, old rusty lock that holds the two old iron gates together. He holds one door and gives the other door a swing. The squeaky old iron gates come to a stop.

"Do I lock them back up or do I leave them open, sir?"

"Leave them, Enrique, we will be coming back this way."

Enrique gets back in, and they proceed down the road. They cross a small but fast-flowing stream with a rocky bottom. As the Land Rover continues, it treks through a muddy trail. Tony notices several buildings. The first one looks like one of the many old buildings they passed on their way to the ranch. It has a mud wall with its roof made from the dry leaves of the palm trees that are so abundant throughout the region. Next, they pass a bunkhouse for the cowboys. It's a more modern building with a green tin roof. Tony notices four or five rockers, a long table made out of rough lumber, with matching style chairs under the same style palm leaf roof. And about thirty feet away, under a tree that looks like a large umbrella, he sees a hitching post with a rusty old water trough.

A short, stocky man with a beard and a large sweat-soaked cowboy hat gallops over as soon as he sees them.

"Patron, how are you, sir?"

Patron is a term used to refer to land owners and Don is used to show respect to a man.

"I am fine, Miguel. How are your wife and the children?"

"We are all fine, patron." He turns to one of the boys riding up from behind. "Quickly, tell your mother that Don Emilio is here and he has a guest. Tell her to prepare lunch for us. Don't forget to tell her Enrique is also here with them."

"Miguel, this is my friend, Tony. He will be staying with us for a few days."

"Miguel Salazar—pleasure to meet you, sir."

"Tony ... ahh, well, just Tony for now, Miguel. It's a long story."

"We can talk about it over at the bunkhouse mess table." Emilio tells them.

"Good!"

"Philippe, get us something cool to drink!"

"Yes, papa."

"Have we lost any more cattle, Miguel?"

"Yes, we lost one last Monday."

"How?"

"It was killed and butchered right on the spot."

"Where did it happen, Miguel?"

"It happened at the big, old dead tree where the river takes a sharp bend."

"I know the spot. Miguel, do you have any idea who it might be?"

"Yes. Fortunately, it had rained, and we were able to follow the tracks all the way to a small house on the outskirts of town."

"We will ride there after lunch."

"Do I send for the local police to meet us there, Don Emilio?"

"No, Miguel, let me speak with them first, and then I will decide what I will do."

"Patron, you have a good heart. I fear sometimes people try to take advantage of this."

"Miguel, if they confuse kindness for weakness, they will find out quickly that I am not a man to be taken lightly. I have always said, 'I say what I mean, and I mean what I say.' I believe in giving everyone one chance, so let's not make an exception with this cattle thief."

"As you wish, patron, now let's see about lunch."

As Tony and Enrique walk to the house, Tony sees two large dogs lying on the front porch of the house. He walks over to the male dog, Tito. As he gets closer, Tito gets up and walks over to meet Tony halfway. Tony begins to pet his large muscular neck. He looks at the scars on his side.

"I bet he's caught a hog or two in his lifetime."

Emilio looks up from his seat at the table. "You know about cattle and you seem to know about hog dogs too."

"I guess so, sir."

"We have too many hogs in this part of the country," Miguel says. "They can ruin an entire pasture over night. We use the dogs to catch them. They are far too smart for traps."

"Have you tried a trap with a rotating door and a live hog for bait, along with corn?" Tony asks.

"No, we have not, but that sounds like something that might just work. Thank you, I will try it at our first opportunity."

"We need to find out about your past, son. You had to have some type of cowboy past or else you must have read a lot of books on hogs and cattle."

"He must be a cowboy," Enrique says. "I can't imagine there are any books on hogs or cows out there with more than four pages."

Philippe, Miguel's youngest son, gives Enrique an inquiring look. "I am sure there are lots books with lots of pages on cows and hogs, too."

Enrique rolls his eyes. "Whatever, little cowboy."

"I will not be a little cowboy all my life. I will soon be a real cowboy like my father."

"Mind your manners, Philippe," Miguel says.

"Yes, Papa."

"I am sure the boy meant no disrespect to Enrique," Emilio says.

Tony asks, "What do you do with the hogs once you catch them, Miguel?"

"Don Emilio has us send the animals to be processed, and then the meat is sent to the orphanage in the nearby town."

Philippe jumps in. "Would you like to go with us on a hog hunt, Don Tony?"

"Sure, Philippe, I would like to see your dogs in action."

"But first we eat," Miguel says.

Emilio, "it a cool day let us enjoy your wife's excellent fried chicken under the shade tree instead of inside."

"As you wish, Philippe help your mother bring the food and drinks"

"Yes, papa"

After a fine meal and some reminiscing on how Don Emilio and Miguel had built up the ranch.

"That was an excellent meal, as usual, Senora Salazar."

She blushes. "Thank you, Don Emilio."

"Philippe?"

"Yes, Father?"

"Saddle Sultan for Don Emilio, and Linda for Don Tony."

"Father, do I saddle one for Enrique?"

"Pleeeease, I'll stay and help your mom clean up," Enrique says.

"Where are we going now, sir?" Tony asks.

"Can you ride, Tony?"

"I don't know. I hope I can. I guess we'll soon find out. Are we going into town to see about the dead cow, sir?"

"Yes, we are."

"Do you think we will have any trouble with the man that stole your cow, Emilio?"

"Don't know, son. If you like, you can stay here with Enrique. I'll understand. This has nothing to do with you, Tony."

"After all you and your family have done for me? What kind of a man would I be if I did not back you on this?"

Emilio puts his arm around Toni's shoulder. "My daughter was right about you, Tony. You are a good man."

Philippe, who has been walking a few steps behind them, smiles and takes Toni's hand.

"Don't worry, Tony, I will take good care of you."

Tony looks down at the little boy in cowboy boots that are clearly two sizes too big for him.

"I feel a whole lot better now, Philippe. Thank you."

Fernando, the middle son, brings the horses, and Tony sees a horse that looks exactly like the carved one in the Milan home.

"He is magnificent! Just like the image in the hallway at your home, sir."

"Yes, he is Sultan a pure breed Andalusia, brought here from Spain. I have had him since he was a baby. I have been offered over a hundred thousand dollars for him."

"Wow, a hundred thousand dollars? That's a lot of money."

"Yes, Tony, but what price can you put on family?"

"I guess none, sir."

They mount up and head down the rocky road. As soon as the dogs see the men mount, they jump up from their afternoon nap under the umbrella tree and eagerly run ahead of the horses. As they cross a small creek, the dogs turn and run toward a stand of palm trees.

"That's where we have been seeing a lot of hog signs, Don Emilio." Miguel tells them as he calls the dogs back.

"Tito, Mancha, come back here. Maybe later you can show Tony how you earn your keep around here."

After about a forty-minute ride, they arrive at a small shack with no glass or screens in the windows. A frail-looking woman in her forties is bent over a bucket full of faded old clothes. She tries to work the dirt out of a little boy's worn and tattered blue shorts. Behind her, on a single clothesline, hang more worn and tattered clothes. She hears the metal clang of the horse's steel shoes on the cobblestones. Looking up, as the cloud of dust from the horses settles around her, she wipes the sweat from her forehead. She is startled to see the four riders now standing in front of her little home. Recognizing Don Emilio, she quickly loses the color in her face.

"Can I help you, Don Emilio?"

"Yes, is your husband home today, Senora?"

"Yes, he is home today and every day. He cannot find work anywhere, Don."

A short skinny man with no shirt or shoes steps out from the shadows. His head hangs low.

"Do you know who I am?" Emilio asks.

"Yes, Don, I do."

"And do you know why I am here?"

"Yes, I do, Don Emilio."

"What did you do with my cow?"

"We ate some. And the rest, I gave to my parents and my wife's brother's family. They also have nothing to eat, Don. Please do not have them arrested. I am the one you want. I am the one who took the cow."

"You killed my cow and carried all that meat by yourself?"

"Yes, Don, I did."

"How many families did you feed with my cow?"

"About four. Will they all be arrested, Don?"

"No one is going to be arrested. If your family is going hungry, you go and see Miguel. He will cut out a cow for you and your family. Then you will help him do whatever he needs done at the ranch in return."

The woman runs to Emilio, who is still atop his horse. She hugs his leg and, weeping, begins to thank him over and over.

Emilio turns to the man. "Do you have shoes?"

"No, Don, we cannot afford shoes."

"Go down to the village and give this note to the man that runs the bodega by the old church. Do you know the one?"

"Yes, Don, I know the one."

"Take your wife and children and get what you need."

"Thank you, Don." The man tells Emilio; he had heard many stories of Emilio's generosity, but still he is not sure he is actually hearing him correctly.

"This is not a handout. I expect you to help at the ranch when Miguel needs you."

"Don Emilio, my family and I will do anything you need at any time."

"Good." He extends his hand to the man and they shake hands. "Good day to you all."

As they turn and ride away, the woman can be heard saying over and over, "God bless you, Don! God bless you all."

As they turn down the gravel road, her voice is drowned out by the clatter of hoofs. Tony breaks the silence.

"Will they help Miguel, if he needs them?"

"Yes they are poor, but a proud people. They will come," Emilio says.

"I am glad you brought me along Emilio."

After riding for about half an hour, Tito catches scent of something. He puts his black nose to the ground and starts off over a small hill. Mancha is hot on his trail. As she catches up, they both go out of sight. She lets out a loud howl.

"Come on, Tony, we must not lose them."

They come up over the top of the hill, Miguel in the lead. Tony can see Sultan's muscles ripple as he digs into the soft dirt and kicks loose mud into Toni's face. All of a sudden, Miguel's horse stumbles in a hole, and he and his horse both go down in a cloud of dust. Emilio and Philippe come up to him first. They get off to check on him.

"I'm fine, stay with the dogs and get that hog," Miguel says.

Tony takes off at a fast gallop, after the dogs, in a cloud of dust. He rounds a small rock outcropping and sees the dogs. His eyes fixate on a very large and angry reddish brown hog. Tito has the beast by the ear, while Mancha barks relentlessly. The minute she sees Tony dismount, she grabs the other ear. Tony rushes up, grabs the hog by its hind legs, and throws the hog on its back. He has flashes back in his mind of a yellow dog running in and also grabbing the hog. He puts his knee on the hog and orders the dogs to let go. Tito is happy to let go and runs to lie down under a small bush; his big red tongue with black spots is panting as fast as he can make it go. He begins to dig a hole under the little tree, looking for some cooler dirt. Mancha is more reluctant to release. Finally, she relinquishes her grip and gives the hog one last nip on the rump before she joins Tito in the shade.

The rest of the men, all arrive together.

"Philippe, quick, get me a rope to tie off his feet!" Miguel shouts.

"Tony, you must have done this before and you certainly know how to ride a horse!" Emilio says.

"I really didn't think of what I was doing. I guess it just came naturally. I guess maybe I have done this before." He pauses. "Where did the yellow dog go?"

"What yellow dog, sir?" Philippe asks. "We do not own a yellow dog."

"I could have sworn that I saw one more dog. A yellow one."

"The dog must be in your mind, Tony," Emilio says. "Maybe it's trying to come back. This is very good. We must have done something to trigger your memory."

"What do we do with the hog now?"

"We'll tie his legs, and Philippe will ride back to the ranch, get the trailer and the other boys. They can come back and load him up later."

"This has been an interesting day. I can't wait to tell Christina," Tony says.

They arrive back at the stables. The smaller children come running to hold the sweaty horses.

Miguel says, "Pablito, remove their saddles and hose the horses down good before you feed them. And don't leave Don Emilio's saddle with the rest. Bring it to the house."

"Yes, Papa."

Enrique, who has been asleep in the old hammock under the two large oak trees, walks over. His hair is all a mess. As he tucks in his shirt, he asks, "Do I make ready to leave, sir?"

"No, you must accompany us for dinner," Miguel replies.

His wife Sara's voice can be heard from the back. "I am making your favorite, Don Emilio."

"Fried pork chunks, Sara?"

"Yes and homemade black beans."

"Sounds good to me. Tony, how about you and Enrique?"

Enrique responds. "Black beans give me gas, but you're the boss."

"It's settled. We stay and ride home with the windows rolled down."

Emilio phones home. "Hi, little one. How was your day of shopping?"

"It was like a day at the office for you, Daddy."

"Then it was a good day and you had fun." They both laugh.

"Do I tell Alva to count you in on dinner with us tonight, or will you be eating with them?"

"The sun sets late this time of the year. We will eat here and head home in time to be there before dark."

"Sure thing, Dad. See you soon."

"Love you, sweetie."

Just then, Tony hears the distinctive clatter of an approaching horse. It's Philippe, returning home.

Tony, "Your horse is very beautiful, Philippe."

"Yes, he is very fast, just like his father, Sultan."

"Sultan is your horse's father?"

"Yes, he is."

"Then that makes your horse very expensive too, correct?"

"Yes, sir, he is."

"Philippe, you were the second to arrive. Are you sure there was no yellow dog that might have left before your dad and Emilio got to us?"

"No, sir, we have the only hog dogs in this area. None are yellow in color."

Just then Enrique walks up behind them.

"Your mother needs you to get something for tonight's dinner."

"Excuse me." He runs off.

"Enrique, how can Miguel afford to buy his son an offspring from Sultan?" Tony asks.

"Don Milan is a very rich man with the heart and soul of a campesino."

"What is a campesino?"

A campesino is a farmer, but also one who is one with the land. Emilio likes to help people, not just use them like his daughter."

"Why do you say that about Senorita Christina?"

"You'll find out one day." Enrique says as he walks away.

Sara rings the large triangular steel frame in front of the house. Tony starts to make his way to the house. Emilio, walking a few steps behind him, notices a handful of chickens running toward the house.

"Look, Tony, even the chickens like her cooking."

"Maybe they are hoping to be invited to dinner Sir."

"I am sure they will all have their turn at the table, at one point or another."

That evening, Emilio, Enrique, and Tony say goodbye to Miguel and his family. The men board the Land Rover for the trip home. As Tony gazes out his window, he reflects on all that's happened in just one short day. He has taken a special liking to Emilio, for the man that he is and the love he has for the people.

"Sir, if I ever find myself in such an encounter as you did today," Tony says, "I hope I have the intelligence and ability to handle it the way you did."

Emilio laughs. "You are a very smart young man, and you showed me today that you are a true friend. Remember, Tony, a man must be true to himself. He must say what he means and mean what he says."

"I will always remember that, sir."

"Does that apply to women, too?" Enrique asks.

"It should my friend," Emilio responds, "but as you know, women are a more complex creature—often more difficult to understand and almost impossible to predict."

"Yes, I know for sure, they can be impossible," Enrique says.

Emilio reclines in his seat, pulls his hat over his tired eyes, and lets the bumpy road gently rock him off to sleep. Tony gazes out his window at the ocean. The sun is beginning to set, making it look like a huge mirror with thousands of little diamonds sending tiny rays of the sun in all different directions. He wonders about his own fate and if he'll ever regain his memory.

They hit a large pot hole and Emilio glances over at Tony. He sees Tony gazing out into the sea;

"She is very tempting."

"I'm sorry, what did you say, sir?"

"The ocean, she tempts men away from their home and family. She can be very beautiful but also very angry and untrustworthy."

Enrique rolls his eyes. "Just like a woman."

"Yes, Enrique, just like a woman."

"I wonder what I was doing out there in the first place." Tony says. "And, what if I had a family and I am the only one to survive? That is what scares me the most. I can only hope I was out there by myself and fell in—or my ship sank and nobody else was out there."

"Son, I can only give you all the resources that are available to me and hope we can bring this to a happy ending for you and anyone else in your life."

"Thank you again, sir. I will never be able to repay you and your family."

Enrique turns and looks at him, wanting to say something more but afraid of the consequences it could bring him. He recalls the last time he and Christina had an argument. Her words still resound in his ears: "My dad will not be running this show forever. You cross me and you will be looking for a new job. Your resume will read 'Gay man with no talent, looking for well-paying job.'" Enrique turns away.

"Mister Tony, I am sure you will be alright."

"Thank you, Enrique."

Two hours later, they find themselves back at the Milano home.

Christina runs up to her father.

"Hi, Daddy, how did it go?"

"It went well."

"Did you find the people who have been stealing my cows?"

"As a matter of fact, I did."

"Good, Daddy. How long will they be in jail?"

"There are not going to jail."

"Did you give away another one of my cows?"

"Our cows, Christina. I'm not dead yet."

"You know what I meant."

"I worked out a payment plan for the cow."

"Dad, what am I going to do with you?"

"Well, how about a big hug for starters?"

"Sure, I can do that."

"And, I think we have a genuine cowboy here."

"Really! Daddy"

"Yeah, you should see him ride and catch wild hogs and—"

"And what, Dad?"

"And help me drink red wine."

"Men, do you ever grow up?"

"If and when I grow up," Tony says, "I hope I turn out like your father."

"Great, now I have two of you to worry about," Christina says.

"Christina, have you asked your mom if she has heard any news of anyone going overboard in Florida? Or of any boats that might have sunk?" Emilio asks.

"Dad that is the first thing I asked Mom when we spoke the other day and again just today. She says she has heard nothing but was going to ask a friend who knows someone in the Coast Guard to check for any missing persons."

Emilio says, "If anyone knows people in Florida, its Christie's mom."

"That sounds good to me. Maybe I have someone looking for me, and they have contacted the Coast Guard."

"You make it sound as if you are not enjoying your stay with us," Christina says.

"I am sure that is not what he meant," Emilio says.

"You are absolutely correct, sir. I am enjoying myself. I just need to know if I have a family that needs me, and is looking right this minute for me."

"I told you my mother is looking into it," Christina says. "What else do you want form me, Tony?" She turns and leaves the room. "I'll see you in the morning."

Tony looks at Emilio.

"I hope I did not hurt her feelings."

"Did I not tell you that women are complex creatures? I am sure she will be fine by morning."

"Good night Tony, I am sure we will both sleep good tonight."

"Yes sir we will, good night."

Chapter Seven
Barbie's Career is Launched

Back in Los Angeles, the day of Barbie's demo has arrived.

"Are you ready to do this, kid?" Karl asks.

"I'm as ready as I'll ever be."

"Okay, Barbie, you are sure you are going to be able to sing this song without coming apart on me, right?"

"I will do my best."

"You mean your absolute best, right?"

"Yes, Karl, my absolute best."

"On three, okay? One, two, three."

She begins her song. Karl is in the mixing booth with the sound engineer.

"When she hits the high note, back off the soundtrack a little."

Engineer, "Hey, this is not my first demo."

"Sorry, man, I'm just a little nervous."

"Aren't we all?"

As she hits her high notes, Karl looks at the producers. They smile and look back at him. *Yes, she did it,* he tells himself. The song is over, and she looks at Karl. He gives her the high sign. She takes off her earphones and lets out a yell. She runs out of the booth and into her mother's arms.

"You were awesome, Barbie."

"Thanks, Mom, and thank you for coming with me."

"I would have walked here to be with you on this day! Besides, you know how I feel about Karl."

"I know, Mom, but he did get me here."

"No, you got you here—with your voice."

"Mom, it takes more than a voice now days to make it in this industry."

Karl walks over. "How about me? Don't I get a kiss and a hug, too?"

"Sure." She hugs him. He kisses her cheek. Barbie pulls away.

"Thank you, Karl."

"I have a good feeling about this kid. How about you and I go out to dinner later to celebrate."

"You mean all three of us?" Barbie's mom interjects.

"Well, Elena, I thought you might be tired after the plane ride and all the excitement of the day. So I was thinking more of Barbie and me."

"Actually, Karl, I am feeling kind of tired, myself," Barbie says. "Can I take a rain check?"

"Sure, doll face."

At the airport the next day, Barbie and her mom are waiting to board the plane. Her phone rings.

"Hello? Hi, Karl. Where are you? What? Oh, my God, Karl!"

"What, Barbie. What happened?" Elena asks.

"Hold on, Mom. Go on. They did? They do? Oh, my God!" She begins to jump up and down in the middle of the hall ignoring people who are walking around her and staring.

"Mom, I got it. I got the recording contract."

They embrace, then hold each others hand and go round and round not giving notice to the people trying to get around them.

Elena calls her husband.

"Tomas, she did it. She got the recording contract. Yes, we just found out, right now. She's on the phone with Karl, right now."

Elena looks up at Barbie.

"When did they call you, Karl?" Barbie asks.

"They just called me right before I called you, Barbie."

Karl smiles and gives the limo driver a wink... Karl had actually known the day before but waited until Barbie and Elena were at the airport to tell Barbie.

"Doll face, I am almost at the airport. I'll be in to see you in a couple of minutes, so stay put till I get there. You can tell your mom to board the plane now, if you like. I'll tell you more in a bit."

"Tell my mother to board without me? Why?"

Karl has already hung up the phone.

"What's going on Barbie? Why is he telling me to board without you?"

"I don't know, Mom, but I am sure he has a good reason."

"Oh, I am sure he has a reason to get me out of here, and I'm sure it's for no damn good."

"Mom, please give him a chance. He has gotten me this far."

As they pull into the terminal, the limo driver smiles and looks at Karl.

"That's one way to separate the calf from its cow."

"You wait for us here, and, as far as you're concerned, that call did come in while I was with you."

"Yes, sir."

He makes his way to the coffee lounge where Barbie and her mom are waiting for him.

"Well, I did it, kid. I got you on your way. How about a kiss?"

She reluctantly gives him a kiss on the cheek. He looks at her mom and smiles. Elena just looks away.

"Just two things, doll face; first, you and I have to stay over for a few more days. And, second, you'll have to take a stage name like we talked about.

"Is that absolutely necessary?" Elena asks.

Karl glances at Elena. "Which one, the name or having to stay?"

"Both, actually."

"Yes, both are a must. Look, I got you this far, Barbie. Either you do as I say from now on or you can get on that plane with your mom and forget everything you have worked for all these years. It's now or never."

She looks at her mom with tears rolling down her cheeks;

"It's now. Karl, on that name thing, Eric and I thought if I had to choose one, then he liked Crystal."

"You and Eric? Well, he is not here, is he? But I will talk to the producers and try to convince them; although, I have to tell you, they were pretty adamant about Safire. I will give it one last try, for Eric's sake."

"Thank you, Karl."

Karl walks a few steps away and dials his cell phone. On the other end, he hears a man's voice.

"Well, hi, son, how are you doing?"

"I'm doing just fine, Dad. How's Mom?"

"Oh, your mom is feeling much better from her knee surgery. She can even get around by herself now."

Karl looks at Barbie and waves his arm, as though he is arguing with someone. He gives her a half smile.

"Your mom is coming now. Would you like to speak to her, son?"

"No, Dad, I'm busy. I'll call her later." He hangs up.

Karl walks back to Barbie.

"Well, I tried, but they are stuck on Safire and they won't budge, kid. The brass at the studio label feels this is the right name for you and your career."

"I guess if that's what they want, then, okay, let's do it," Barbie says.

"Oh, your mother will have to fly back. We can't let the public see the next rising star with a chaperone, right."

"I guess not."

Just then, her mom returns from the rest room.

"Well, Barbie, can you keep your name?"

"No, Mom, they want a stage name."

"Can you take Crystal, like Eric wanted, then?"

"No. I will take Safire and see where that leads me."

"Your dad will not be happy."

"I know, but I don't have a choice."

"Do what you feel is best, but you will always be Barbie to me and your dad."

"One more thing, Mom."

"Don't tell me I have to change my name too?"

"No, Mom." They both laugh and hug.

"No, but you do have to fly home without me."

"Why can't I stay and help you get organized?"

"No, Mom, you have to fly back."

"It's that damn Karl, isn't it?"

"No, I have an image now, and I can't go around with a chaperone."

"I am no chaperone, Barbie. I am your mother and don't you ever forget that."

"Mom, I know, and I love you and Dad more than words will ever say. I have to do this for me, for us and, maybe, if I become famous, I can find Eric or he'll find me."

"Do what your heart tells you is right, Barbie. We will always love you, and we will always be here for you, too."

Their conversation is interrupted by an announcement over the PA.

"Air West Flight 813, departing for Miami, Florida, now boarding at Gate 3."

"That's you, Mom. I love you. Call me when you get home."

"What about you?"

"Karl had to call someone, then he is going to meet me downstairs by the limousine, we need to back to the recording studio to sign some papers.

They hug one last time and both turn away with tear-filled eyes. Barbie looks back one more time as her mom disappears into the line of passengers now boarding. She turns and makes her way to the arrival gate to wait for her limousine.

While she waits for the limousine she calls Javy.

"Hi, Jav."

"Hey, girl, how did it go?"

"I did it, Jav. I got the recording contract."

"Yee-haw! You hear that, Maxx? She did it. Your mom is now a rock star. Do I have to take Maxx to one of those fancy doggie hair salons now?"

"Yeah, maybe they can give you a haircut, too!"

"No way, girl, only Deana, that red-headed, blue-eyed Amazon at the Hair Hut can cut my hair. So, what's next, Barbie?"

Well, it's not Barbie anymore."

"What name did you settle on?"

"Safire. Do you like it?"

"Safire sounds hot."

"Yeah, I guess that's why they wanted it."

"What did your dad have to say about the change?"

"Mom is going to break the news to him when she gets home."

"Oh, boy, I can just see your dad now."

"I am not a little girl anymore. I have to make choices and decisions that I may not be crazy about, but, nonetheless, I have to make them in order to further my career."

"I am very happy for you, Barbie. You have all my support and Maxx's too."

"How is Maxx doing?"

"He just lies around. I took him on a run yesterday, but you can see his heart's not in it. He is beginning to eat a little more, but it's the same thing when I take him for a walk. It's as if he has someplace to go, and I have trouble bringing him home."

"I'm sure he'll come around. Karl is on the other line.I have to go. Give Heather my love. I will keep you guys informed on what is happening. Love you both, Bye."

"Bye, Barbie, and good luck."

She hears a honk and turns to see the limo, as she steps off the curb Karl gets out, he opens the door she gets in and they drive off.

As they sit in the back seat of the limo. Karl tells her of his all plans to make her rich and famous and how one day the whole world will know her name. As he speaks and goes on and on with all his thoughts and plans, she looks out the window and thinks of just one dream. The dream that one day she will again, be reunited with her one true love Eric.

Chapter Eight
The Fire

Several weeks have passed. Tony comes down to have breakfast and finds Christina and Emilio already at the table eating.

"Good morning, all."

"Good morning, Tony. How are you today?"

"I feel just fine, sir."

"You need to be less formal with me."

"Yes, sir, I know."

Christina, "Who knows? Someday you might even call him Dad, too." Tony just smiles.

"Why don't you kids come down and have lunch with me at my office today?"

Sounds good to me, Daddy—I need to do some shopping anyway."

"Then it's a date. I'll see you kids later."

Emilio kisses Christina and walks down the stairs to his car. Tony and Christina walk across the courtyard.

"Tony, are you ready to go do some shopping?"

"Well, I thought maybe I could hang out at the beach while you shopped."

"And have you sitting there just watching all the girls go by? No way!"

Tony stops walking and looks at her. She now realizes she might have gone too far. She smiles at him.

"Then take Enrique with you. He knows everybody on the beach."

Enrique mutters, "Everybody except the women."

Just then her cell phone rings.

"Hi, Daddy, did you forget something?"

"Yes, Christina. Is your mom back from her vacation in Las Vegas?"

"Yes, Dad, I called her last night. They had just gotten in and they were unpacking. She sounded pretty tired. She said she would call today."

"Good, I'm glad to hear she is safe at home again. After two weeks in Las Vegas, I'm sure she's worn out from shopping."

"Is there something you would like me to ask her, Dad?"

"Yes, as a matter of fact, she never told us what her friend at the Coast Guard said."

"I'm sorry, Daddy, she called me a few days after she spoke with him and said they had heard nothing at all. I should have told you, but I did not want to upset Tony."

"Thank you baby; you are a good daughter, Christy."

"Thanks, Daddy, I love you. Bye."

Alva is cleaning the kitchen cabinets when the phone rings.

"Hellow Milan residence. O hi how are you today, Mrs. Jennifer?"

"I am fine, Alva. And you and your family?"

"They are fine. Would you like to speak with Christina or Don Emilio?"

"Christina, please."

"Let me go get her. I think she is about to leave with Tony." She puts down the phone and runs outside.

"Miss Christina, phone. It's your mother."

"Tell her to call me on my cell." She looks at Tony and turns to Alva.

"Never mind, I am coming. Tony, please wait for me. I'll be right back."

"Sure thing. I'll be here in the shade with Enrique."

"Hi, Mom, you feeling a little more energized today?"

"Christina, you have no idea, of the kind of running around I have been doing! It sure was tough." She laughs.

"If I know you, some fun was had along the way too, Mom."

"Maybe, just a tad. Christina, you mentioned your young man. How are things going with him?"

"Mom, that's what I need you to find out for me."

"Me, how?"

"You remember that private investigator that you used to check your present hubby?"

"Yes. Hector."

"Mom, do you still have his number?"

"Yes, I still have his number."

"Just in case, Mom?"

"Hey, if I have taught you nothing else in life, it's that you should always have your bases covered."

"That's why I'm calling the master."

"I know, sweetie."

"Daddy would have a fit, Mom. You must promise me you will not tell him a thing."

"Done, but if this young man has a prison record ..."

"Stop, Mom. He has no record, I am sure of that."

Well, send me all the information you have on him. I will get Hector on it at once."

"Mom, can I just talk to Hector myself?"

"Sure, I'll look up his number and call you right back with it."

"Thanks, Mom. I have to go, so just call me on my cell and leave the number. You're the greatest. Bye, Mom."

"Bye, sweetie." She hangs up.

As the Land Rover pulls around front, Jose, the gardener, jumps out of the driver's side.

"It's all yours, Enrique."

Enrique jumps in, turns up the radio, and turns to Tony.

"Is Her Majesty on the way?"

"Enrique, sometimes I sense some hostility between you two."

"I am not allowed to speak on that, sir."

"This is between you and me—no one else."

"Mr. Tony, she is cunning, cold, and can be ruthless to get what she wants. Her father has given her everything ... except a heart and a conscience."

The front door opens, and Christina steps out, wearing a stunning yellow dress with a matching hat and purse. She makes her way toward them.

"You two aren't talking about me, are you?"

"No, Enrique was telling me about the jungles of Costa Rica."

"The only thing he knows about the jungles is how to stay out of them. Drive, Enrique."

"Yes, ma'am."

"May I say you look stunning?"

"Yes, you may, Tony."

Just then her cell rings. She looks at the number.

"Aren't you going to answer that?" Tony asks.

"No, it's just my mom again."

Tony looks at Enrique, who quickly looks away.

They are making their way through the city streets, when they hear a fire truck coming up behind them. Enrique pulls to the side of the road. The large red truck screams by, siren blaring and air horn blasting. Its flashing red lights are barely visible in the large cloud of dust following it as it roars down the cobblestone street. Enrique pulls out slowly and begins to follow it, keeping a safe distance behind. All of a sudden, Toni's facial expression changes.

"Step on it, Mike!"

Enrique turns and looks at Christina.

"Step on it, I said!"

"Step on what, sir?"

"Damn it, step on the gas, Mike!"

"Do as he says!" Christina says.

They come to an intersection.

"Clear."

"Clear what, sir?"

"Clear on right, damn it. Mike, go, go, go!"

Enrique floors the SUV and holds on with both hands. They turn another intersection.

"Clear right." Eric yells out again.

This time Enrique floors it. Without hesitating, he cuts the wheel hard, and a gust of wind blows Christina's new hat out the window. Through the rear-view mirror, Enrique can see it floating behind them. The hat gently lands in a large mud hole just a few feet off the road. With a big smile on his face now, Enrique blows the horn. He urgently yells at an old man who is pulling an old fruit cart to get out of his way.

The car's engine comes alive as it screams down the street behind the fire truck. Tony reaches over and blows the horn.

"Move out of the way," he yells out the window.

Turning the next corner, they arrive at an abandoned building. Tony reaches over to Enrique's side.

"What do you need, sir?"

"The radio! Where's the radio?"

Not knowing that Tony is looking for a two-way communications radio, he responds, "In the dash, sir."

"Never mind."

Tony jumps out. The firemen are setting up their hoses. One goes to the front door. He tries the door handle and finds it locked. He goes back for an axe. Tony sees that smoke is venting out of the top floor of the building. As it leaks out of the crack near the roof, it is sucked quickly back in. The fireman now makes his way past him with axe in hand.

"No, you can't open that door!" With a startled look, the fireman pulls away.

"What? Please, sir, step out of my way."

"No, you cannot open that door! Look, look up there. Do you see that?"

The fireman now realizes that a back draft situation is at hand and what will happen if he opens that door.

"You have to ventilate, at the top." Tony tells him

"Yes, sir, you are correct."

The police have now arrived. One of the officers takes Tony by the arm.

"Sir, you must step back and let these men do their job."

At that moment, he snaps back.

"Yes, I'm sorry." Puzzled, he holds his head with both hands. "I don't know what came over me."

"You were amazing, sir!" Enrique exclaims. He is tempted to say something more but is interrupted by Christina's order.

"Let's go now. My father is waiting."

In the car, Enrique grins.

"I can't believe the way I was driving. I felt like a real firefighter. I wish we could do it again."

"Just hope my father does not find out."

The color drains from Enrique's face.

"I take full responsibility for what happened here today," Tony says.

"That is very noble, Tony, but it was Enrique behind the wheel. But, not to worry, this will stay between the three of us, I promise."

They arrive at her father's office.

"Hi, Teresa, is my daddy in?"

"Yes, take a seat. He is with his accountant. I think they are almost through." She buzzes the intercom. "Sir, your daughter is here."

"Tell her I'll be right out." The door opens and Christina's father walks out.

"Hi, kid, how was the shopping?"

"Boring, as always. Right, Enrique?"

"Yes, Senorita."

"Then, let's go. Maybe I can spice up your day. You like seafood, Tony?"

"Yes, sir, I sure do."

"Well, you're in for a treat then."

"Teresa, I am going to step out with Tony and Christina for lunch. Don Antonio will stay here to do some work on my accounts. Please don't let anyone bother him."

"Yes, sir."

"Let me get my cell phone and then we can leave. Teresa, can we bring you back anything?"

"No, thank you, Don Emilio. I brought my lunch."

"May I use your rest room before we leave?" Tony asks.

"Certainly, Tony, right down this hall. It is the second door on the left. Christina, next time you call your mom, ask her to call me when she has a chance."

"Sure, Dad. You're not afraid to call her yourself, are you, Daddy?"

"No, but I do need to talk to her."

"Why, Dad?"

"Well, I was thinking, she has a lot of so-called friends. Maybe she can use one to help locate some information on Toni's real identity."

"Good idea, Dad. I will ask her for you, next time we speak."

They walk outside to a bright and breezy day.

"What a beautiful day!" Tony says.

"If you like our climate so much, then you should consider staying in Coast Rica, Tony."

"Well, Christina, I would and maybe I will, but I do have to try and find out who I am and were I'm from."

"I am sure in time, it will all come back," Emilio says.

"I hope so, sir."

They get in the Land Rover and head out to the restaurant. They pass a site where they are breaking ground for a new hotel.

"What are they going to build here?"

Enrique replies, "They are going to 'Eric-t' a new hotel."

Christina's face flushes red with anger. She glares at Enrique. He knows that he has angered her and turns and looks away.

They make their way down to a line of small buildings that end a few hundred feet from the gently pounding surf.

"Father, you and Tony go ahead. Enrique and I have to have some girl talk."

"Sure, honey."

After they are out of sight, she turns to Enrique.

"What the hell was that?"

"What do you mean, Christina?"

"You know damn well what I mean. You called him by his name, when you said 'Eric-t.'"

"I did?"

"How do you know his name? And don't even try to lie to me."

"When Alva went to make your bed, she found the wallet on the bed and looked inside and saw his name. She also saw the picture of the girl with him."

"If you mention this to anyone, so help me God you will never work in Costa Rica again. As for Alva, I will deal with her later. About the girl in that picture, my mother had her investigated. She is an old girlfriend from high school. Now, let's go."

"Yes, Senorita."

Tony and Emilio stand before a rustic-looking building with old, weather-beaten wooden tables. The windows have no glass. Instead, they have a large wooden awning held in place by a wooden post on each side. They walk inside and find a room full of similar tables. An old ceiling fan is turning slowly creaking at every other turn. A white and yellow cat lies quietly at one end of the rustic bar.

"Don Emilio, how are you today?" says a voice from behind the bar.

Good, Alfredo, and yourself?"

"I am fine, Don." A large, middle aged lady walks in from the kitchen, whipping her hand on her apron.

"Hello, Don, how are you today?"

"I am doing just fine, Nancy."

"So, this is the famous restaurant you spoke of this morning?" Tony asks.

"Yes, this is my favorite restaurant."

Just then Christina and Enrique join them.

"Well, what do you think, Tony?"

"I will let my taste buds do the judging."

"That's my boy."

"Can we sit outside, Daddy? It's cooler out here."

"Whatever you say, Christy."

"May I suggest the sea food soup, today and the grouper is fresh, as always," Alfredo says.

"How about a large order of seafood soup for all?" Emilio says. They all agree.

After lunch, Emilio looks at Tony. "Well, Tony, what do you think of my little hidden treasure? Is that not the best soup you ever had?"

"It was very good. I seem to remember someone making a similar soup, but I can not remember who."

"Maybe it was your mom," Christina says.

I don't know, maybe it was—or, I hope, still is."

"Dad, I would like to walk with Tony over to the old marina. After Enrique drops you off, he has some grocery shopping to do for Alva. I can call him to pick us up when he's done."

"It's alright with me, if that's what you want."

She looks at Tony.

"Sure sounds interesting to me, Christina."

Emilio bids them good-bye, and he and Enrique drive off.

As they walk out the back door, Christina takes off her shoes.

"Come on; take off your shoes, Tony. We can cool our feet in the surf."

He takes them off and begins to walk alongside of her.

"Look, Tony! What a neat-looking seashell. Please get it for me."

He bends over to pick up the shell, and Christina suddenly kicks up water in his face and takes off running.

"Hey, you!" he yells, as he runs off after her.

She stops and turns suddenly, and he runs into her arms. Putting his arms around her waist, their eyes meet. She slowly moves her lips to his. As they start to kiss, he pulls back.

"I can't do this."

"Why not?"

"I don't even know my name. For all I know, I might be a married man."

"I am sure you're not."

"How do you know?"

"We women know these things. Besides, you were not wearing a ring."

"I still can't do this. I need time to see if I can remember who I am."

She turns and walks away.

"I've changed my mind—let's go home."

"Look, Christina, I am sorry, but I am thinking of you. What if you fall in love with me and I have someone else?"

"I am already in love with you—can't you tell, Tony?"

"Yes, I can, but please give me a little more time, for both our sakes."

She turns and retrieves her cell phone. "Enrique, Come get us, now."

"Can I pay for the groceries first, Senorita?"

"I said *now.*"

"Yes, Senorita. I am on the—" Enrique hears the phone go dead.

A few minutes later, Enrique pulls up to the little restaurant where they had lunch. Christina walks to the front passenger door, gets in, and slams the door behind her. Tony gets in without saying a word.

"Do we head home, Senorita?" Enrique asks.

She gives him a cold look. "What do you think?"

Enrique turns the car around, and they head home without saying a word.

When they arrive back at the Milan estate, Christina walks inside and sees Jose, the gardener, sitting down drinking a soft drink. He jumps to his feet.

"Find Alva and tell her I want to speak with her right now."

"Yes, Senorita, right away."

Tony does not want to upset her any further. "I will be in my room if you need me, Christy." She does not answer him.

Alva walks in from the kitchen. She is drying her hands on her apron.

"Senorita Christina, your mother called. She said to call her at her beach condo tonight."

"I need to see you in my room, now."

Alva follows her upstairs. Christina walks into her room. As soon as Alva enters behind her, she slams the door shut. Tears were already rolling down Alva's face, as Enrique had run in through the back door and had already warned Alva of the pending firestorm.

"Who the hell gave you permission to go through my things?"

"Senorita, I am so very sorry, but I was not going through your things. I was doing my job and—"

"Your job is not to look at my personal belongings."

"I am sorry, but I thought the wallet belonged to Mr. Tony."

"Did you look inside the wallet?"

"No."

"Liar, I know you looked inside."

"Yes, but I did not mean to."

"Shut up. If this ever happens again, you will be out of a job faster than you can say *San Jose*. And, one more thing, you saw nothing—you understand me? Nothing at all!"

"Yes, I understand. Please forgive me."

"Get out of my sight."

Christina picks up her phone and calls her mom.

"Hi, Mom. I called Hector, but all I got was his machine."

"Christina, I spoke with Hector's brother. He is in Delaware on a job. He will get back to you as soon as he gets home."

"Thanks, Mom. I'll talk to you later then."

"How about your father? How is he lately? You know, he never calls me. Christy, does he ever ask you about me, honey?"

"No, Mom, not really."

"Oh, well. Good-bye then."

"Good-bye, Mom."

Chapter Nine
Karl Shows his True Colors

The weeks have turned into months. Barbie is now known as Safire and her singing career has taken off. She has a new release and is part of a tour that will take her to twenty-two cities. She is currently in Atlanta. Passing time before her performance, she stands on the balcony of her luxurious hotel suite, looking out over the city. She sees all the city lights and the lines of cars headed to the sports auditorium where she will be performing later that night. She wonders if today is the day Eric will be in the crowd.

There is a knock at the door. It is the security guard.

"Miss Safire, a young man is out here to see you."

Her heart leaps, and she drops the glass of orange juice from her hand. It hits the floor, sending shards of glass all around her bare feet. Not thinking of the glass, she runs to the door.

The security guard, having heard the noise, shouts, "Are you alright in there?"

She grabs the silver door handle and flings the door open. Standing next to the security guard is Javy and his girlfriend, Heather.

"Is everything alright, Barbie?" Heather asks.

She wipes the tears from her face. "Yes, I am fine. Please come in and sit down. Can I get you guys something to drink? And, no, Javy, I don't have any beer."

"Hey, Barbie, if you're short on cash, I can spot you a few bucks for beer."

"Stop playing around, Javy. Barbie, is everything really alright?" Heather asks again.

They walk out to the other balcony while Javy looks for something to drink.

"Be careful, Heather, I dropped a glass over there."

"How did that happen?"

"When you guys knocked, I was looking at all the people out there, here to see me. The only person I really want here isn't here. I just thought it was him when you knocked. And, well, it wasn't."

Just then Javy returns with a soda.

"Thanks! I drive for eight hours to hear you sing, and this is what I get."

"Javy, you know what I mean. I feel so lost without him."

"I know, Barbie, but you have to perform for these people. You know I love him like a brother, but you must face the fact he may never come back."

She turns to him, tears now running down her rosy cheeks. "Don't say that."

"Of course, he'll come back," Heather says.

"I'm sorry Barbie, your both right." Not knowing what else he can say.

"He will come back. I know it. I feel it. He's out there somewhere, and we will be reunited."

She runs to her bedroom.

"What were you thinking, Javy? She has to perform in a few hours."

"Do you think it's easy for me? Eric and I grew up together, and I am closer to him than I am to my own brother. But it's been months now with no word—nothing. It's like he never existed. I hate to say it, but it would have been better for her and all of us if they had found a body, or a least his life preserver."

"Javy, she believes he is alive. She says she can feel it. How do you know she is wrong? You even tell me that Maxx just sits and looks out the window all day long."

"Yeah, but he's just a dog, Heather."

"Animals can sense things we can't, Javy. Who's to say they couldn't both be right?"

"I hope they are both right, but it's harder and harder as the days go by to imagine ever seeing him again."

Just then the front door opens. Karl walks in.

"Where's my girl?"

"You don't knock?" Javy says.

Karl walks by them as if they aren't there.

"Where are you, doll face?"

She walks out, her eyes still puffy.

"I'm right here."

"Have you been crying?"

"No."

"No? Well, it sure looks like it to me. Have you forgotten you have an audience that has come from miles away, many from other states, just to see you?"

"No, I'll be ready. Don't worry."

He turns to Javy. "This is your doing, isn't it?"

Heather stands in front of Javy and puts her hands on Javy's chest. "Honey, please, don't."

"I *do* worry," Karl says. "Do you have any idea how much time I have put into this concert?"

Javy, "Then maybe *you* should go out there and sing."

Their eyes lock. "I think you two should leave now."

"These are my friends, and they have come a long way to be here with me today," Barbie says.

"You have a lot of new friends waiting to hear you sing. You need to be at your best," Karl says. He smiles. "Tell you what, doll face. You get ready, and I'll take them with me. They can be in the front, so you can see them and they can enjoy the concert, on me. Now, you go and get ready, the limo will be here soon to get you."

She turns to Javy. "You heard the man. I do have to get ready. We can talk after the concert."

Barbie kisses Heather and Javy, and they walk out to the elevator with Karl. The elevator doors open, and they step inside. Karl turns to them.

"I have a lot of money and time invested in her, and I am not going to let you or anyone ruin it for me and her. Here's fifty bucks. There's a cowboy bar just down the road. Go have a good time on me. Then go home and stay out of her life."

Javy gets in his face. "I knew her when she was in grade school, and I love her like my own sister. You are not going to keep her separated from us."

Heather pulls on his right shoulder.

"Calm down Javy."

"I don't have to keep her from you. Her new career will do that for me," Karl says.

The elevator doors open. Karl walks out and turns to them, holding the doors open with his foot, as he puts the fifty dollars back in his pocket.

"She's not in grade school anymore. You're part of her past. I am her future. I am not going to let you ruin this or any other concert for her." He lets the doors close behind him.

In the elevator, Javy says, "That good-for-nothing son of a—"

Ding! The doors open and an elderly couple walk in.

"Calm down, Jav. We can see her after the event."

"Good thing we have our own tickets. That son of a—"

The elderly lady looks at him. The door opens and they all walk out.

At the concert that night, Barbie is scheduled to be the second entertainer to sing, due to her being a rising star. Karl is standing with the band manager and the sound technician.

"Man, she's on today, eh, Karl?" The band manager tells him.

As he looks out into the crowd, Karl grins.

"Yea she is, she may not be the main headliner here tonight, but by this time next year she will be, and nobody or nothing will keep me and her from getting there."

As Karl walks away, the band manager looks at the technician. "I guess he's not about to let that little golden goose fly away."

After she performs her last song, Javy looks over at Heather. "Do you want to stay for the rest of the concert?"

"Whatever you want, Javy." Knowing he no longer wants to be there.

"Heather, let's go. I want to speak with Barbie before she heads back to the hotel."

As they making their way slowly through the crowd, they reach the backstage entrance. Javy looks at the security guard, as he pull the plastic pass from his jeans pocket, "I have this pass from Safire to go backstage and see her."

The security man looks at the pass. "Yes, sir, right this way."

Just then, a man in a black suit with a two-way radio steps in front of them. He looks at their pass; he then takes it and puts it in his coat pocket.

"I am sorry, sir, you cannot go backstage to see her and I have to keep this."

"What? I got that a pass from Safire herself. Look, see she singed it."

"Yes, I see it, but I have orders not to let anyone pass and keep this."

"Who gave you those orders?"

"I am not at liberty to say, sir. She will be signing autographs after tomorrow's concert. You can see her then."

"I have to be at work on Monday in Florida. We are leaving tomorrow at noon."

"I'm sorry, those are my orders and there's nothing I can do."

"Sir, are you sure someone has not made a mistake?" Heather asks. "We have been friends of hers form back in grade school."

"I am absolutely sure, Miss. Now, you have to go, so please don't make a scene."

"Scene?" Javy says. "You tell that good-for-nothing Karl, I know this is his doing."

Two police officers are now standing behind them.

"Is there a problem here?" One of the officers asks.

"No, there is no problem. We are leaving," Heather says.

The second officer says, "Good, we will escort you out then. This way, please."

"I don't need a damn escort," Javy says.

"Please, Javy, let's go," Heather says. "We don't need any trouble, and we don't want to wind up in jail in Georgia."

The first officer looks at Javy. "That's good advice, sir. You should take it."

"Let's go, Heather. I don't want to spend another day in this town."

Back stage…

Karl knocks on her dressing room door.

"Who's there?"

"It's me doll face, can I come in?"

"Just a minute"

"You knocked them dead, doll face."

"Was I that good?"

"You were phenomenal." He puts his arms around her.

"Karl, please."

"Kid, I have you on the fast track. People are clamoring to see you, and I can't even get a small kiss?"

"Sure." She kisses his cheek, but he turns quickly and their lips meet. She pushes him away.

"You can't push me away forever. Eric is not coming back. You have to face the facts and move on."

"He is not dead. I know it, Karl."

"Then why hasn't he come to see you? People are coming from all around to see you. Why isn't he out in the crowd? Why hasn't he called? Against my advice, you've kept your old cell phone number, and everybody in your past calls you, except him."

"I like the people in my past. They are like family."

"Like Javy?"

"Yes, like Javy."

"You cannot let someone come in and upset you like they did before your performance. You must decide today, Barbie. Is it going to be Barbie and her friends from the past—or Safire, the number-one future rising star in the country, and me?"

Just then her cell phone on the table rings.

"Leave it alone. Let it ring. Now, let's go. I have a big celebration planned for you at the Garden House Restaurant, and you don't want to be late for your celebration."

"How about Javy and Heather, Karl? Did you invite them?"

"I mentioned it to them in the elevator, and I sent one of the security people to pick them up after the concert, but he reported back that he could not find them. Doll face, you know Javy. He might not like that type of environment. In fact, he was asking me, in the elevator, if I knew how good that cowboy bar down the street was. He's more blue jeans and cowboy boots, Safire. You know that."

"He is, but you did give him the option to come with us, right?"

"Doll face, would I lie to you?"

"I guess not."

"I'll tell you what, Safire. If it makes you feel better, I'll carry your phone for you. This way you can have fun, and, if someone important to you calls, I'll make sure you get the call. Deal?"

"Yes, Karl, deal."

"Go and change and I'll wait right here for you."

"I'll only be a minute."

While she is getting changed, Karl picks up her phone from the table.

Karl opens it up and sees she has a message and two missed calls from her mom. He listens to the message from Javy; then he erases the message and shuts off the phone, and slips it into his coat pocket.

"Who was it that called me Karl?"

"Just your publicist, he wants to make sure you are on the way to the restaurant and your big celebration."

"I am ready now, let's go."

"You might as well stop calling her number, Javy. You left her a message. She'll call us back, I'm sure," Heather says.

"Sure, if that rat, Karl, doesn't get to the phone first and erase my message."

"You really think he would do that, Javy?"

"Oh, for heaven's sake, Heather, wake up."

"Javy, do you want to try and see her one more time tomorrow, before we go home, or do you really want to go home now?"

"No, let's go home. If I run into Karl one more time this week, I will probably wind up in jail. I'll wait for her to call. He can't keep her from us forever."

Chapter Ten
Christina's Plot

Christina picks up the phone and dials. "Hi, Mommy, what's new? Have you got good news for me?"

Yes, as a matter of fact, Hector sent me his report today."

"He was supposed to contact me, Mom."

"Yes, he called, but you were out."

"Well, don't keep me in suspense! Tell me everything."

"Hold on, Christina, let me see. Where do I start? Let's see. He is, or was, a firefighter. Actually, he's a lieutenant here for the city of Hialeah.

Christina already knew he was a firefighter having seen his badge in the wallet.

"A firefighter you say mom, I told you he was no criminal mom."

Now, on his marriage status let me see. It's here somewhere."

Christina clenches her teeth. "Mom, stop playing around and tell me right now."

"Easy there, sweetie. He is not married."

"I knew it, I knew it!"

"But, Christy, he does have a girlfriend."

"Yeah, but he's not married, Mom."

"Listen, he might not be married, but his girlfriend is that new singing sensation, Safire."

"Mom, stop playing around."

"I am not kidding! He is, or was, her boyfriend."

"He *was* hers. Now he's mine."

"Christina, do you hear yourself? You know the right thing to do here is tell him the truth, and if he chooses you, then he's yours."

"No, Mom, he's mine now, and I'm not going to give him a chance to go back to her."

"You do as you wish. I'm just telling you, he might regain his memory. Then what are you going to do?"

"The doctor said he cloud regain his memory at any time or stay like this forever, if it's forever it will be fine by me, and if he finds out, well if we're married, then I don't think we will have a problem."

"Christina, you know I am not one to preach, but you really need to think this one through."

"I have, and my mind is made up. It was made up the first time I laid eyes on him."

"What about *his* mind? Is it made up, too?"

"Leave that to me, Mom."

"Christina you are acting like child and you are not one anymore. This is like the time you wanted a horse like your fathers and Emilio had to travel to Spain and pay ten thousand dollars to get you one." "By the way what ever happened to that horse?"

'He acted up one day and I sold him to a neighbor for five hundred dollars."

"Five hundred dollars! Your dad paid more than that for the shipping alone."

"What will you do if Tony acts up? He is a man and if he finds out you lied to him, I am sure there will be hell to pay then."

"Mom, I'll cross that bridge when and if I get to it."

"Christina, I did my part. The rest is up to you. But if this backfires on you, don't say I didn't try to warn you."

"Sure thing, Mom. Just do not say a word of this to Dad."

"Not to worry. I don't have anything to say to him, and I am sure he doesn't want to talk to me either."

"Hold on a minute, Mom, he just walked in. I'll ask him now." She turns to an empty chair in her bedroom. "Daddy, its Mom. Do you need to talk to her?"

"He said no, Mom. One last thing, Mom. I need Hector's phone number."

"What for?"

"So I can thank him."

"I already did that, when I paid him."

"Mom, give me his number again."

"Hold on a minute. You have a pencil and paper?"

"Yes."

"Alright, here you go." She gives her the number.

"Thanks, Mom. Bye, Mom."

"Bye, baby."

Another week rolls by. Christina's plan is in full swing. Tony and her dad have become very good friends. Emilio has become very fond of the young man and is about to become an unwilling participant in his daughter's scheme to marry Tony.

Christina goes to see her dad at his office. He looks up from his work when he hears her voice.

"This is a very pleasant surprise."

"Are you busy, Daddy?"

"I'm never too busy for my girl."

"Daddy, how do you feel about Tony?"

"What do you mean?"

"Well, how would you like him as a son-in-law?"

"I like him a whole lot, but we still don't know anything about him or his past."

"Dad, he has lived under our roof for six months now. If he was an axe-murderer, I think he would have killed someone by now."

"Yes, but what if he's married?"

"And what if he's not, Dad? He could stay like that for the rest of his life, married or not, and I really love him."

"Does he love you?"

"Yes, he does."

"But, Christy, I have never seen him so much as to try to hold your hand."

"He is shy, Dad, but I know he loves me. He's told me many, many times. But he is afraid you will not approve. He feels that you think he is not good enough for me."

"That's utterly ridiculous. You know I don't look at people like that."

"I know, Daddy, but he doesn't know you like I do."

"What do you want me to do?"

"Talk to him, Dad. Tell him he might never regain his memory and how we would like him to stay here with us. You could offer him a job with you and tell him how much you need a junior partner. He would be perfect for the job."

"I got him a job with my good friend Don Fernando's warehouse, and he is doing very well, from what I am told."

"But, Daddy, that's a job. You can offer him more than just a job with you."

"Are you asking me to try and buy him into marring you?"

"No, Dad, he already loves me. This is just so he could feel like he is contributing more."

"Contributing more to what?"

"Oh, Daddy, pleeeeease."

"Tomorrow is Saturday. I will speak to him then."

"You're the best dad any girl could ever hope for."

"Well, then, let me get back to my work. Tell Alva I will not be home for supper."

"Is something wrong, Dad?"

"No. Well, maybe. I have to speak with Captain Hernandez about one of the motors on the *Christina M,* and I have a dinner appointment with a client."

"Is there problem with the ship, Dad?"

"She's a female, and you females are always giving me one kind of trouble or another. Bye, sweetheart."

"Bye, Daddy."

Captain Hernandez arrives at Don Emilio's office later that day.

"Mercedes, you are looking beautiful as usual. How are you feeling today?"

"Captain Hernandez, you are such a charmer. I am doing fine. And you?"

"Good for an old man. Is Don Emilio in?"

"Yes, he is expecting you. I'll tell him you are here."

"Thank you, Mercedes."

"Don Emilio, the captain is here."

"Tell him I will be with him in a minute."

"Please, have a seat, Captain. He'll be with you in minute."

After a few minutes the intercom rings.

"He will see you now, Captain."

"Thank you, Mercedes."

"Captain, how are you?"

"I'm good. And you?"

"Couldn't be better, captain. Step into my office and have a seat."

"Now, Captain, what do you think is the problem with the ship?"

"On our return trip from Miami, Pedro noticed the number-one engine running hotter that usual."

"What do you think it can be, Captain?"

"It could be a bad thermostat or a clogged radiator."

"Well, what do we do now?"

"I flushed the radiator and replaced the thermostat. Maybe we should take her out for a few hours and see how she runs."

"Captain and in the worst-case scenario, what could be wrong then?"

"The worst case could be a small crack in the engine block, and that would be covered under warranty. But it would mean cutting out the floor to remove the engine block, so let's hope it's not that."

"Let's hope not, Captain. Let me look at my schedule. Maybe we can take her out for a trial run before Christina's birthday."

Emilio looks at his calendar, "I don't think I can fit that in."

"Do you think she will be in good enough condition to take her out for Christina's birthday next week, Captain?"

"I don't see why not. We can stay out a mile or so. We can just run up and down the coast and stay in close enough to run in on one engine, if necessary."

"Alright, we will test her then, Captain."

"Good, Don Emilio. I will make plans to fuel her up on Friday and be set for the party on Saturday."

"Good."

"Don Emilio, where does time fly? How old will she be?"

"She turns twenty-three. Can you believe that?"

"Don, I remember when she was just a skinny teenager."

"Time is passing us by, my good friend. Thank you for coming, Captain. We'll be in touch. You have a good day."

"You too, sir."

"Oh, by the way, Captain, did the Coast Guard report any missing boats in the area where you picked Tony up?"

"I don't know. Senorita Christina told me she had contacted you and that you had called the Coast Guard from here."

Emilio stands up his face now red with anger.

"Aah, yes, that's right, Captain. I completely forgot. I did call. I will speak to you later."

"Good bye, Don Emilio."

Emilio walks out of his office and slams the door. "Mercedes, I am going home for the day."

"But, sir, you have two more appointments today and a dinner appointment with Don Pedro Cruz tonight."

"Please call them to reschedule and give them my sincerest apologies."

"Yes, sir, have a good weekend, sir."

"You, too."

Emilio drives up to the front of the house and sees Alva and Enrique unloading groceries.

"I will move the van out of your way so you can park, sir," Enrique says.

Emilio steps out and slams the door.

"Never mind. Is Christina in?"

"Yes, I think she is." He opens the front doors.

"Christina, where are you," he yells out.

"I wonder what the princess without a heart has done now." Enrique mutters.

"Hush, he might hear you."

"Yeah, God forbid he hears someone tell him the truth about his darling daughter."

From her upstairs bedroom, Christina yells, "Daddy, you looking for me?"

"Yes, I sure am. What the hell were you thinking lying to Captain Hernandez? Worst of all, lying to your own father?"

"Dad, let me explain."

"Explain? There, could have been more people out there. Did you ever consider he might have had his entire family out there in a sinking boat?"

"Dad, it was a misunderstanding between the captain and me. I told him I was going to notify you first, to see if you wanted to call the Coast Guard or let him call them from the boat."

"Christina as a captain, he could lose his license for doing something that irresponsible and I could get in trouble, too."

"Dad I know that, I told Pedro to have the captain call you. With all the excitement he must have forgotten to tell the captain. I'm sorry he didn't do it, Daddy—I should have made sure he did. It's my fault, Daddy, for not following up on Pedro. You know next week is my birthday, Daddy, I'll be very sad if you are angry with me."

"Christina, don't ever let this happen again."

She kisses him and gives him a hug.

"I love you so much."

"I love you too, but sometimes, Christina, I don't know what I am going to do with you."

"Maybe I need a man in my life, to keep me out of trouble?"

"Maybe you do. At any rate, I am getting too old for this, for sure."

"Maybe, Dad, you could speak with Tony about me."

"And tell him what, Christina?"

"Tell him that it's alright with you if he is interested in something more serious with me."

"Christina, I have no problem with him, but I am not so sure he is as in love with you as you are with him."

"Dad, he does love me. He has told me many times. It's just that he is afraid you might not think him worthy of me."

"That is absurd. You know I do not judge anyone, although I would just like to know at least a little about his past."

"I know, and so would I. But, Dad, I don't want to lose him either."

"So, what do you want from me, Christy?"

"Dad, I know Tony is a little intimidated by all you have."

"There is nothing I can do about that, Christina."

"I know, but maybe if he had a better job, then he would feel he could offer me a better lifestyle."

"Again with this, we spoke of this not long ago, and you know how I feel, I got him a job at Don Fernando's warehouse. What else can I do for him?"

Knowing from the past, that if she continues he'll give in.

"Daddy, he has an office job taking orders at the warehouse and making sure the trucks are loaded. That is not much of a job for the man who is going to marry Emilio Milan's daughter, now, is it daddy?"

"There are many men that would love to have his job. But what's on your mind, daughter?"

"Daddy, you are always saying you are not getting any younger and you can't be in two places at one time."

"Yes, I have said that. Now, what's your point?"

"Well, Daddy again, I think you need a junior partner. One who could help run all your interests and give you time to spend with your grandchildren."

"Grandchildren? Aren't we running before we walk, Christina? I will think more on this, but as I told you before, I will not offer any man a bribe to marry my daughter."

Just then, Tony, having heard Emilio's voice, walks out of his room.

"Emilio, how are you today, sir? Is everything alright?"

"Yes, Tony, Daddy and I were just talking about my birthday and how to spend it. Do you have any surprises for me on that day, Tony?"

"I do have to have Enrique drive me into town, if that's alright with you, Emilio?"

"Sure, Tony, whatever you need."

"Do you need to know my ring size, Tony?"

"Actually, I was thinking of a bracelet."

"Oh, well, I have lots of bracelets … but as you wish, Tony."

The next morning, Emilio comes downstairs for breakfast and finds Christina, Tony, and Enrique in the kitchen.

"How is everyone today?" Emilio asks.

"We are all fine, Father. And you?"

"Good. Enrique, will you bring the Land Rover to the front door for me, please?"

"Yes, sir."

"Are you going somewhere, Daddy?"

"Yes, I am."

"But, Daddy, I thought you wanted to speak to Tony?"

Emilio gives her a stern look. "Yes, I had forgotten." He turns to Tony. "Do you have a minute?"

"Yes, I do," Tony replies.

"Let's go sit by the pool."

"I'll go put on my bathing suit and tan while you men talk," Christina says.

Emilio and Tony go out to the pool and sit under a large green umbrella.

"Tony, do you think you would like to stay here in Costa Rica?"

"I think I would, but you know I still don't know who I am."

"Well, my daughter and I like who you are, and I would like to offer you a permanent position with me in my company."

Christina comes out in a black bikini and sits a few feet from them in the sun. Tony can't help but look at her as she walks by him.

"She is a very beautiful woman, isn't she, Tony?"

"She is that, sir."

"Enrique, bring the radio and set it up for me," Christina says.

"Yes senorita."

"How do you feel about my daughter, Tony?"

"She has a lot to offer any man, and the one who can win her heart will be a very lucky man, I feel."

Enrique, who has just finished setting up the radio, rolls his eyes.

Christina is on her cell phone with her friend Tina.

"Senorita, would you like to hear a new CD I just got?" Enrique asks.

"Sure, play it and let me see what she sounds like."

He cuts the plastic wrapping, opens the new CD, and hands Christina the plastic cover so she can look at the face of the new rising star. Enrique puts the CD in the player a pushes the play button.

"Tony, do you love my daughter?" Emilio asks.

"Sir, I can only—"

Before he can finish the sentence, he is distracted by the soft and somehow familiar voice now coming from the CD player. Toni's face transforms. He gazes out toward the ocean and then slowly turns and looks back at the CD player sitting on the table.

"I think I know that voice?" Tony says almost in whisper.

Christina who is twirling the plastic CD cover while talking on the phone is not paying attention to Tony or to the music. Suddenly she looks up and sees Toni's face then it hits her. She looks down at the cover and it's *her,* the girl in the picture with Tony. She drops the phone, leaps out of her chair, and rips the cord to the CD player from the wall.

"What happened? I like that song … or at least I think I do," Emilio says.

"I can't stand her, Dad. I hear it's not really her singing the song anyway."

Tony asks what her name is.

"Safire," Enrique says. "She is the hot new singing sensation from Miami."

Christina snaps, "Don't you have a car to bring for my father?"

"Yes, I am on my way."

"Tony, you are so silly," Christina says. "Of course you know the voice—you heard the CD three days ago. Enrique played it on our way to see my dad."

Enrique, walking away, looks back at her. He knows she is lying, because he purchased the CD the day before and he can't help but wonder why she is making that up.

Emilio says, "Tony I have a ten o'clock appointment. I will be taking the *Christina M* out for Christian's birthday. We can finish our conversation then."

"Yes, sir."

"And, Tony, give some thought to what you and I talked about. I am in no hurry, so take your time and think it over."

"I promise I will, sir, and thank you again for all you have done for me and for this opportunity you are offering, which I will not take lightly."

Enrique goes to Alva's room. He knocks on the door.
"Yes?"
"It's me."
"Hold on, I am getting dressed."

"Oh, Alva, it's me, Enrique. I don't care if you're naked."

She opens the door. "What's so important that it can't wait until I get dressed?"

He tells her what just happened.

"So, what's your point—she didn't like the CD?"

"No. You said there was a picture of a young woman with Tony."

"Yes, I did. So what? Oh, you don't think that girl in the CD and Tony are acquainted, do you?"

"I don't know, Alva, but I aim to find out. Do you remember what she looked like?"

"Not really. The picture had gotten wet and was kind of blurry. Come on, Enrique, you can't really believe they knew each other, do you?"

"I don't know, but why would she react like that, Alva?"

"I don't know, nor do I want to find out. You know good and well how she can act and react to things."

"I have an idea, Alva."

"You are not going to get me in trouble with her again, are you, Enrique?"

"No, forget it. I have to think more on this."

"She will have you fired if you meddle again, you know she will."

"You know what, Alva? I have had enough of her, anyway. If it happens, it happens."

"Enrique, there was one more picture, but I heard her coming up the stairs, and I did not get to see it."

"Alva, you go in her room all the time. If she was going to hide something, where do you think she would hide it?"

"She may be mean and cruel, but she is not good at hiding anything."

"Go on please, Alva."

"Enrique, if you tell anyone what I am going to tell you, I will tell everyone you know I caught you looking at me naked."

"You made your point—now, tell me quick."

"She hides it in a shoe box in her closet."

"Alva, she has lots of shoes. Which one?"

"She has lots of shoes, dummy, but only one shoe box."

"I got you now. Look out your window. Are they still by the pool talking?"

"Yes, but I want no part of this."

"Just look out the window. If she starts up this way, call my cell."

"I swear, if you get me fired, I will move in with you. Make sure you are not caught, Enrique."

Enrique makes his way out to the hall and sets out for Christina's room while Alva takes her position by the window.

Christina approaches Tony, who is still sitting by the pool.

"I couldn't help but overhear some of the things my dad said to you. I did not know he was going to talk to you about me and you, but I was very glad to hear what he had to say. You know, I have very strong feelings for you, Tony, and you must decide one way or another if you do or don't love me. If you don't, then I am sure my father will ask you to leave here. And I hope Don Fernando, your boss, does not get mad at you and fire you when he finds out you broke my heart."

"That's not meant to be a threat, is it, Christina?"

"Of course not. What kind of a person do you think Don Fernando is?"

"Sorry! If I could only find out once and for all if I have ties to someone or somewhere else. Then, if not, I will stay here."

"I understand, Tony. I have to call my mother back. I will be right back."

She gets her sunglasses and heads for her room. Alva sees her and runs for her cell phone. She punches in Enrique's number and, as the phone rings, she whispers, "Pick up, pick up, Enrique." She is horrified to hear an electronic voice say, "All the lines are busy, please try your call again."

She is now in a panic and runs to the door. Swinging it open, she now realizes that in all of their planning, she has forgotten to get dressed. She can hear Christina walking up the stairs. Just then Enrique comes running out of Christina's room, pushes Alva back into the room, and closes the door behind them. Alva flops down on her bed.

"I swear you are going to give me a heart attack!"

"Never mind that. Alva, it *is* her!"

"Who's her? What are you telling me?"

"The girl in the picture, it's Safire. I am ninety-five percent sure it's her. I saw the picture of them together. They were younger, but I am sure it's them."

"Okay, Mr. Detective, what next?"

"I don't know, but I will come up with something. You can count on that!"

"The only thing I count on is that we will both lose our jobs if she ever finds out."

"You know what, Alva? It is what it is."

Christina walks by Alva's room not suspecting a thing. She steps into her room and calls Hector Diaz.

"Hello. Hector Diaz here."

"Yes, Mr. Diaz. It's me, Christina Milan. We spoke earlier."

"Yes, I remember now. What can I do for you?"

"Well, I need you to get me some type of identification for a person from as far away from Florida, if possible."

"What you need, I can provide, but it will be expensive."

"I did not ask you for a price, did I? I asked if you can do it."

"Oh, I can do it."

"How does California sound?"

"That sounds perfect. I'll get on it right away."

"I need this here by this Friday."

"That will cost extra. You're only giving me six days."

"You asked me again about the money. Are you the right person for this job or not, Mr. Diaz?"

"Yes, I am."

"Then don't worry about the money."

"You can call me at this number, and your money will be there as soon as I get my papers."

"Good-bye Mr. Diaz."

"Good-bye, Miss Milan. And good luck on your project."

The following Saturday afternoon, plans are being made to celebrate Christina's birthday on the *Christina M* the next day. Alva is busy cooking and making last-minute preparations—ordering refreshments and instructing the bakery on what time they need to be at the ship with the birthday cake.

Enrique is making preparations of his own. He has read every article he can find on Safire, but nowhere is there any mention of a man in her life or that she has been in any type of boating accident. He decides he will give his CD one more chance. Maybe it will spark some emotion or jog Toni's memory. He places the radio of the Land Rover to play the CD ,puts in Safire's CD and leaves it all set up to come on at a flip of the switch .

Don Emilio is making last-minute phone invitations for the party on Sunday.

"Alva, have all the preparations been made?"

"Yes sir, everything has been taken care of."

"Thank you. Well then, let's get this show on the road."

They walk out of the house just as Enrique brings the Land Rover to a halt at the front door. Tony sits up front, and Emilio and Christina sit in back. They start making their way down the winding road that leads to the marina. Enrique sees his opportunity and quietly turns on the radio. As soon as the music begins to play, Christina taps Tony on the shoulder, at the same time she pushes the down button on her window.

"Let me see that CD. I want to see if there's a song on there that I like."

"Christina, I thought you said you didn't like her?"

"Did I say that dad?"

Tony hits the eject button, and the CD pops out. He hands it to her. She turns it from one side to the other. Her gaze meets that of Enrique, who is looking at her through his rear view mirror. She lets the CD slip from her fingers and it fall out of the window.

"Oops! I am so sorry, Enrique."

Enrique brings the car to a sudden stop and jumps out the driver's side. He finds his CD on the side of the road. It has a small crack in it. He walks back and gets behind the wheel without saying a word.

"That was so clumsy of me! I will buy you one to replace it. I tell you what—I'll get you two CDs of that male singer you think is so hot. What's his name again?"

Enrique says nothing. He just drives to the marina. The plan is to spend the night on the ship and get an early start the next day.

At the marina, Emilio introduces Tony to the crew.

"This is Captain Hernandez. He was in charge of the ship when you were picked up. Over here is Pedro. He and Enrique pulled you out of the water. This young man is Fernando. He is the third member of the crew."

"I have no way of thanking *all* you people for saving my life."

"If there is one person you owe your life to, it's Enrique," Captain Hernandez says. "He's the one who saw you floating and had Alva alert me."

Tony turns and looks at Enrique.

Putting both of his hands on Enrique's sholders. "I am sorry I never thanked you. I never knew it was you, Enrique."

"It's alright. I am just glad we were able to save you. And, I must admit, it was exciting to pull you out of the water and to ride the skiff with the motor maxed out like that. I'll never forget that day"

"Max!" Tony exclaims.

"Yes, he maxed out the motor in a hurry—to get you back."

"No, the word *max.* I can't explain it, but I believe I know someone with that name."

"Maybe it is a friend of yours, sir?"

"Maybe, I just don't know. Maybe it will come to me later."

They board the ship and settle into their quarters for the night and await the morning with anticipation.

Sunday's dawn breaks with a light wind from the south and a friendly sky. The guests have all arrived, and the ship heads out to sea. After several hours of fun-filled chatter and sunbathing, Alva's voice is heard over the ship's loudspeaker.

"Don Emilio and Tony, please come down to the main deck so we can sing 'Happy Birthday' to Christina, and she can open all her gifts and cut the cake."

After all the gifts have been opened and the cake cut, Christina approaches Tony, who is leaning against the ship railing and looking down into the churning wake of the propellers.

"A penny for your thoughts?"

"Oh, hi, Christy."

"Thank you for the lovely necklace, Tony. I love it … but I was hoping for an engagement ring."

"Christina, why did you tell me you were the one who spotted me in the water?"

"Who have you been talking to, Tony?" Her smile now gone.

"The captain said it was Enrique."

"The truth is both of us spotted you, but that is really not important. The important thing is that you were saved, and now you are here with me. Tony, will you make this the best birthday of my life and tell me you love me?"

"I do love you, but if I have someone else, how would you deal with that?"

"What if I told you I know you are from California, Tony?"

Tony straightens up." What did you just say?"

"How do you know where I'm from? And why have you waited until now to tell me? I can't believe this. You knew where I came from all along?"

"No, I didn't. Calm down and listen to me. When we took you to the hospital, we did not look in your pants pockets. At the hospital, they took your pants and put them in a plastic bag. They did not notice for days that there was a wallet in there. When they finally noticed, instead of calling me, they sent it to our family doctor. His secretary put it in a drawer and forgot all about it. She found it Friday, while looking for something else."

"With something this important, why didn't she call you or your dad?"

"It is not her place to call us, but she did call Dr. Fuentes. He was at the hospital, and she left him a message. He didn't get it until that night, and it was late, so he decided to wait until now to tell us."

"So you just found out?"

"Yes, Dr. Fuentes just told me a few minutes ago."

"A few minutes ago, I am going to talk to him right now."

"No, you can't. You will embarrass him in front of my dad, his wife, and their children. It's not his fault. I will handle this for you, Tony. But you must promise me something, here and now."

"Sure, Christina, what do you want?"

"Promise me you will never tell a soul about this. Especially not my father. It would be very embarrassing for the doctor, and he is more than just a friend to my dad."

"Yes, I promise never to say a word to anyone. Can we get the wallet tonight?"

"No, Tony, I will go to his office tomorrow and pick up the wallet and have it here for you when you get home from work. But, Tony, will you promise me that if I help you go to California, and we cannot find anyone or anything that ties you there, will you come back here to me forever?"

"I promise you I will." They kiss.

At the bridge, Captain Hernandez looks at the ship's gauges.

"Cut her back, Fernando. The temperature is running too hot on number one again."

The loudspeaker comes on.

"Don Emilio, would you please see the captain."

Emilio walks onto the bridge. "Is there a problem, Captain?"

"The number one engine is still running a little hot."

"Should we return, Captain?"

"I think it best that we do."

"Okay. Turn back and make plans to have it checked out as soon as they can schedule her in at the marina."

"Yes, sir. I'll call them right now."

They arrive back at the marina. The guests begin to depart. Some of the ladies decide to take one last photo as a reminder of the day. Ramona, a longtime family friend, has had one too many.

"Girls, let's take one last picture in front of the boat!"

She takes off her big brown sunglasses and matching hat and bends down to place her drink and scarf on the pier. When she stands back up, she gets too close to the edge of the pier, loses her balance, and falls into the water.

"Dad! Tony! Quick, come help! Ramona has fallen into the water!" Christina yells.

Tony is inside the boat helping Enrique put the leftover cake in a box. He drops the cake, kicks off his shoes, and runs to the edge of the water. Pedro, who was only a few feet away when she fell in, is already in the water and pulling her to safety. A small crowd has formed.

"Quick, somebody grab her hand!"

Tony takes one hand and Dr. Fuentes takes the other. She is pulled up and out. Now on the pier, she begins to hyperventilate. Dr. Fuentes takes her hand and tells her, "Breathe normal again, now. Just breathe. Breathe again. That's it. Breathe again."

Tony, who is standing over her now, stares at Ramona. Upon hearing the word breathe, breathe again his mind drifts back to a young boy lying on the floor of a pool and a girls voice saying "breathe, breathe again."

Ramona's husband, who had gone to get their car, has heard the screams and now sees Ramona lying on the pier. As he runs up to see what has happened, he bumps into Tony, bringing him back to reality.

Enrique, who is standing next to him asks, "Are you alright, Tony? You seem as if you are in a trance of some sort."

"I don't know, Enrique. I don't know what's happening to me."

Ramona is now relaxed and breathing normal. They all have a good laugh.

Emilio says, "We'll see you all next year. Thank you for coming. I hope to see you too, Ramona."

The next day, Tony is getting ready to head off to work. He has been up most of the night wondering what he will find out about his past. Before leaving, he softly knocks on Christina's bedroom door and whispers. "Are you up yet?"

A groggy voice from inside answers. "Who is it?"

"It's Tony. Can we speak?"

She puts on her nightgown and opens the door.

"Are you looking for an early birthday gift of your own?"

"No. No!!!"

"You're not interested?"

"Don't take it that way, Christina. I just couldn't sleep last night, thinking of what we might find. I can't go to work. I need to go with you to the doctor's office and get my wallet."

"No, you can't. We already discussed this on the boat."

"What do you mean I can't go?"

"Tony, this is a very difficult situation for the secretary—it could cost her more embarrassment than it already has."

"Well, I'm not going to tell anyone else."

"Tony, please let me handle this. You know how much I love you. I could have easily gotten the wallet and just thrown it away."

"You could have, Christina, but why would you do something like that?"

"Tony, I love you, and I want you to stay, but I would not do anything that would keep you from loved ones or stand in your way if you have someone else. That's why it is so important to me that we go to California and spend as much time as you think we need to look for your past there."

"You are a good woman. If I cannot find a reason to stay in California, then I know my future is here with you, Christina."

"Now, go to work, Tony, so I can get back to my beauty sleep."

He gives her a kiss.

"Good-bye. And thank you for all you have done for me."

She smiles. *You'll never know the half of it.* She locks the door and heads back to the bed. But instead of getting into bed, she reaches under it and pulls out a brown package that was delivered the Friday before her birthday party. She cuts open the top and looks through the articles Hector has sent along with instructions on how to doctor them.

Miss Milan,

I hope these will help you with your project. You mentioned you will be soaking the articles in water. You must make sure to distort certain parts of the documents so they cannot be traced. The Social Security card is a fake number so make sure you distort the first five numbers and the name. Also, remove the flight number on the airline ticket from California to Florida. On the voter registration, leave the very top that shows the county and state. I did not get you a driver's license. Because of the way they are made and the plastic, it would be almost impossible to distort the picture or the information. I got you something better. I sent you a picture of a group of boys standing in front of an orphanage. Make sure you do not distort the name of the orphanage; it burned to the ground along with all its records, so it will be a great dead end for you.

I sent you a boat-rental agreement. When you go to the boat-rental place, ask for John, the owner. He will recall that when your friend came in and rented the boat, he was alone. He will tell you the police and Coast Guard did an all-out search for him but called it off, after the boat was found floating at sea. Make sure you ask to use the rest room and leave him five hundred dollars under the trash can there.

I hope this helps you in your project. Four thousand dollars will help me in mine.

Hector

She unfolds the documents and begins to carefully soak only the parts of the document that Hector has instructed her to.

There is a knock at her door.

"What?"

"It's me, Alva. Will you be coming downstairs?"

"No. Bring me my breakfast in here."

Alva returns with her breakfast and knocks again at her door.

"May I come in?"

"Wait a minute." Christina opens the door. "Put it on the table."

As Alva walks in, she looks at the bathroom and sees the documents scattered on the floor. Without saying a word, she walks out and closes the door behind her. When she gets back to the kitchen, she sees Enrique eating his breakfast.

"I just came from her room. You should see what she's got going on."

"What, is she smashing more CDs?"

"No, she has papers scattered all over the bathroom floor and a small plastic container of water and her blow-dryer. What do you think she's up too, Enrique?"

"I don't have a clue, but I'm sure it's nothing good."

Later that day, Tony arrives home early from work.

"Alva, where's Christina?"

"I think she is by the pool."

He runs out to see her. "Did you get it?"

"Get what, baby?"

"Christina, stop playing around! Did you get it?"

"Have I ever let you down, Tony?"

"No, you haven't. Now let me see it."

"It's upstairs in my room."

"Well, let's go."

"You're in an awful hurry to get me into the bedroom today!"

He starts off without her.

"Alright, wait up! After all, it is *my* bedroom, for now. Soon it will be ours, right?"

"Yes! Now, let's go."

They walk into the room, and she retrieves the wallet from her purse.

"Here you go."

He grabs the wallet from her hand and fumbles through all the articles she has neatly placed there for him to find. Not saying a word, he goes through them one at a time.

"I can't understand why there is no driver's license in here."

Maybe you had it with your money and it all fell out.

"That could be." He removes the picture of the boys in the orphanage. "This picture seems a bit damp."

"Let me see it. It has been in the wallet for a long time, Tony, so it might have retained some moisture".

"Christina, do any of these young boys resemble me?"

"Actually, this one here does resemble you a bit."

A sad look comes over his face. "Do you think I might be an orphan? I was hoping to have parents and maybe a brother or a sister. It's kind of sad to think I might not have any one out there."

"You can't say that! You have me, and I will always be here for you."

He hugs her and gives her a kiss on the neck.

"How will I every repay you and your father for all you have and are still doing for me?"

"I know how you can make me and my dad very happy."

"I told you on the ship that, if I am not committed to another woman and have no family elsewhere, I will stay."

Finally he opens the boat rental agreement. Tony, "At least this is legible, I will call them tomorrow."

"No, Tony these things are better done in person"

"You are right, but how, this company is out of Miami?"

"I will speak to my father, and we can take the *Christina M* to Miami. We must start there; we will go to the boat rental place first, then to California."

"Your mother lives in Miami, do you want to spend some time with her before we star for California?"

"No we must not waste any time there. I have made arrangements to have a car waiting for us at the dock. After we go to the boat rental we will drive north to West Palm Beach and rent a motor home there for our trip west."

"Drive to California? We can take a plane from Miami to California, Christina."

"No, Tony, I am afraid of flying. Besides, this will give us more time to be together. We can see more states this might help your memory. We can speak with my dad right now. I hear him downstairs."

They find him in his study.

"Dad, can we speak with you?"

"Sure, what's on your mind?"

"The hospital called." She looks at Tony and winks. "They found Toni's wallet. "Show it to him, Tony."

Tony hands over the wrinkled wallet.

"They just now found it?"

"Never mind that, Dad. The important thing is that now we know where he's from."

"California? Is that where you think you're from?"

"I don't know, sir. Maybe."

"That's a long way from here."

"Yes, Dad. We would like to go and see if he has any family over there."

"You said *we,* Christina?"

"Yes, I want to go too."

"You can help him all you want with this, but you are not going to California with him."

"Why not?"

"I will not have my daughter traveling to California with a man. I am old-fashioned, and I will not have everyone in Costa Rica saying that my daughter is off to the U.S. with a man who might already be married. I am sorry, Tony, but I have her honor to think about. Besides, you are afraid of flying. How were you planning to get there?"

"I thought we could take the *Christina M* to Miami and then rent a car or maybe a motor home. That way we could see some of the other states, and that might help jog his memory too."

"First of all, the *Christina M* will be in dry dock for at least thirty days."

"Dad, what if I take Alva and Enrique as my chaperones? We can take the cruise ship from here to Miami and then drive."

"Christina, it sounds like you have this all planned out."

"Daddy, it's the only way we can be sure, once and for all."

"Let me think on it, and I will give you an answer in a day or two."

"Pleeeease, Daddy? You know how much this means to me!"

"I said I will think about it."

Christina and Tony walk out of the study together.

"Christina, what if Alva and Enrique don't want to go on the trip with us?"

She laughs. "Don't worry about that. I have no intention of taking them with us. Just as soon as we get to Miami, I will put them on the next plane home."

"But your dad!"

"My dad needs to realize once and for all that I am not a little girl anymore, and I don't care what people here think or say about me."

With that she turns and walks away leaving him there in the hallway.

He turns to walk back to the kitchen and then sees Enrique at the end of the hall. Enrique looks at Tony and walks away without saying a word. Tony is sure he heard them talking, for the first time he begins to wonder about Christina, could she be as cold hearted and cruel as Enrique says she is. Has his gratitude to her and her father for what they have done for him made him blind to the real Christina? He thinks of how she told him that *she was* the person that saw him and saved him from the sea, never once giving any credit to Enrique. For the first time in many weeks he feels alone and lost, but something in his heart tells him this will all end, he can only hope it is soon.

Chapter Eleven
A Star is Born,
a Past Must be Forgotten

Safire has been on tour for over ten weeks now. She is scheduled to go home for two weeks before she heads out again. She is sitting by the hotel pool in Santa Monica California, twirling the engagement ring Eric gave her on her birthday and staring out at Santa Monica Bay. Karl walks up behind her.

"Hey, doll face, what's on your pretty mind today?"

"I was looking at that small object in the water and thinking what if that's Eric out there, trying to make his way back to me."

Karl rolls his eyes. "Look, doll face, there are three things here that are for sure. First, this is the Pacific Ocean; he was lost in the Gulf of Mexico, so you are talking thousands of miles from here. Second, that object out there is a jet ski, and it is headed away from us. Third, and lastly, Eric is dead and not coming back. You need to face that reality once and for all."

"How can you be so cruel, Karl, as to say that?"

"I am not being cruel, Barbie, I am being realistic, and you need to be realistic too. You know that I have been very patient with you on this Eric thing, but it's time you come to your senses and realize he is gone forever."

"Karl, you know Eric meant everything to me."

"Eric might have meant everything to you as Barbie, but he is gone and so is that little girl Barbie. You are now Safire, and I am now your future. You can no longer live in the past or shut me out."

"Please, I need more time, Karl."

"More time for what, Safire?"

"You are asking me to forget, in eight short months, someone who was a part of my life for over ten years."

"Ten years or twenty, don't you see, it doesn't matter? He's gone and is never coming back; you need to get that through your head once and for all?"

"What do you want from me, Karl?"

"I want you to let me into your life once and for all. After your up and coming open-air concert in Miami, you need to let me in as more than just your manager."

"Karl, I don't know if I can."

"Well, Safire, if you don't let me in after the concert, then you can let me out of your life altogether, for good. You can forget about me and all my contacts once and for all."

"Karl, you can't do that to me—after all we have been through."

"No, Safire, I am not doing this to you—you are doing it to yourself."

He gets up from the table and walks away. He turns to her again.

"Remember this after the concert. It's me and the future or Eric and the past. The choice is yours."

As she sits wondering what she will do about Karl's ultimatum, a young girl taps her on the shoulder. "Miss Safire, may I please have your autograph?"

She takes the pen from the girl and begins to write. The girl's father joins them.

"I must commend you and whoever your managers are, Miss Safire. Only a few months ago, I had never heard of you. Now you are all that my daughter and her friends can talk about."

She thanks the man and then turns and looks at Karl who is walking back into the hotel.

On the plane heading back to Miami, Karl looks over at Barbie.

"I need you to relax for a few days before your first big solo performance at an open-air venue at the Miami Beach seaport. There will be boats coming and going behind you while you're singing. If you don't put Eric out of your mind once and for all, you might fall apart right in front of all the fans who come to hear you sing, not to mention all the ones watching you on TV. You don't want that, do you, Safire?"

"No, I don't, but—"

"But nothing. It's over, here and today. Do you understand? Your whole future is at stake here."

"Yes, Karl, I understand. Have you gone over the songs with Scharla Nelson and the other producers to see what they want me to sing?"

"Yes, we have, and they and I want you to sing 'Breathe Again.'"

"'Breathe Again'? That was our song. I promised Eric, that if I ever made it and had my first TV performance; it would be the first song I would sing for him. You can't possibly ask me to sing it without Eric here?"

"We can and I especially am. This is the only way you will break with your past."

She turns from Karl and just stares out of the airplane's window.

They arrive back home in Miami to a large crowd of fans at the airport. As their plane taxis to its arrival gate, Safire turns to Karl.

"I would like to spend time with my family and friends."

"You can spend time with your family, but try to limit your time with Javy and people who can put you into a depressed state again."

"Karl, you cannot ask me to turn my back on people I grew up with. They are a part of me and who I am."

"No, they are people you knew and maybe needed as a child. But you are all grown up now. You are a star and, as such, you can no longer hang on to these childhood friends. You need to move on and make new, more important friends."

"You are wrong about that Karl. I will never leave my friends behind or change them like they were a set of used tires."

"I am not telling you to forget them completely, Safire. Just keep a little distance from them for a while. Let me introduce you to new and more interesting people who can have a positive effect on you, not a negative one. After your tour is over, you and I are going to sit down and talk about you and me."

"Karl, please not this again."

"I am not asking you to marry me, not for now anyway. All things will come in time. But you have to let me into your life as more than just your manager."

"Karl, you have to give me more time."

"Sure, I will give you more time. I'll give you two whole days after the show. After that, your time is up. You can choose to let me in as more than just your manager, continue with me and your tour, or you can chose your old friends and keep dreaming of a miracle and the return of Eric. We can go our own separate ways."

Just then, the pilot announces they have arrived and thanks the passengers for flying with Air West. As soon as the seat belt sign goes off, Barbie jumps to her feet and makes her way to the exit door. No sooner is the door open than she hurriedly makes her way down the boarding ramp and out into the airport lobby. As she steps out, she sees her mom.

"Barbie, hi, baby!" Her mother runs past security and hugs her. Karl catches up to them.

"Hi! How are you doing, Mom?" Karl asks.

"I am fine, Karl. But I am sure you know that I would have to have been pregnant at the age of nine to be your mom."

"I'm sorry. I meant that in a loving, family way." He turns to Barbie. "I have work to do on your event, Safire, so I'll catch up to you later." He kisses her cheek and walks away.

"Mom, where are Javy and Heather?"

"Javy is still upset over what happened in Atlanta. Heather called your cell and it was disconnected."

"What happened in Atlanta, Mom?"

"Barbie, you don't know what Karl did to Javy and Heather?"

"No, Mom, I don't."

"He wouldn't let them see you backstage."

"No, Mom, he would not do that. He knows how I feel about them."

"Maybe you should talk to Javy and Heather for yourself."

"I will. I'll go see them tomorrow. Now, let's go see Dad and the rest of the family."

The next day, Barbie and her mom arrive at Javy's house. The minute Barbie steps out of the car, she sees Maxx by the living room window. Upon recognizing her, he immediately begins to jump up and down, barking incessantly.

Kiko Garcia

Javy is out back working on his truck. He walks around to the front and sees Barbie and her mom. She runs and hugs him.

"Why did you stay away yesterday, Javy?"

"We wanted to see you, but after what happened in Atlanta, we were not sure you wanted to see us."

"I swear I had nothing to do with any of that, Javy. And it will never happen again." She hugs him again. "Now, let Maxx out before he goes through the roof."

Javy walks to the front door and lets Maxx out. He runs and jumps all over her and then stops and just looks at her. He runs to the edge of the property and looks off into the distance as if expecting Eric to follow.

"He's like this every time I take him out. It's as if he wants to walk and walk and walk. I feel bad bringing him home, but how far can we walk?"

Barbie kneels down and holds Maxx by his massive head.

"Look at me. You have to stop. We both have to go on. It's over, Maxx. We have to mend our hearts and go on from here."

Maxx pulls away and runs into the house.

"He'll be alright, Barbie, but how about you? Will you be alright?"

"I have no choice, I must go on. In a few days I am giving a special outdoor performance at Miami Beach, and I want you and Heather there in the front row."

"Are you sure we will be allowed in this time? I almost went to jail last time we went to see you perform."

"There will be no repeat of what happen to you and Heather in Atlanta I guarantee it Javy."

"I'll tell you what—you can come and you can even bring Maxx. How's that?"

"We have a date." He tells her as he gives her a big hug.

"Now, let's go inside—it's too hot out here."

Chapter Twelve
The Voyage Home

Two days after speaking with her dad. Tony and Christina are sitting by the pool, when Enrique arrives home with four boarding passes to the *Emerald Princess*. Don Emilio has consented to let Christina go with Tony to California.

"I purchased these, as instructed by your father, and we will have two cabins," Enrique says. "One is for you and Alva. One is for Tony and me."

"We'll see about the sleeping arrangement," she says as she winks at Tony.

"Your father agreed to let you go, and I am not going to betray his trust in me and you," Tony says.

"Whatever, Tony," Christina barks back.

Alva brings them some drinks.

"Can I ask a favor of you, Senorita Christina?"

"What now, Alva?"

"When we get to California, can I call my niece? I have not seen her in four years, and now she has a one-year-old baby girl of her own. I would like, if possible, to see them both."

"You and Enrique will be on the first plane back to Costa Rica from Miami. This is not an employee vacation."

Alva turns and walks away. As she passes Enrique, he can see the tears now running down her cheeks. He can't help but say, "Too bad I couldn't have bought you a heart along with the boarding passes." He tells her as he walks away.

Christina glares at him. "Don't you ever talk to me like that and walk away before I finish talking. I'll deal with you when I get back from California."

"Was that necessary?" Tony asks.

"These people take advantage of my dad and my money."

"You mean *your father's* and your money, correct?"

"You know what I mean, Tony. You have to put the help in their place or they will walk all over you, just like they do my dad."

"I disagree. I have never seen anyone walk all over your dad. But he does treat them like family, not mere employees."

"My dad has his ways, and I have mine."

"I see that." Tony starts to walk away.

"Tony, this is not the United States. Here, a woman must be strong to keep what she has. She needs a strong man at her side. Are you that man, Tony? Can I trust you with not only my heart but with all that I own?"

"I do not know if I am the man you need at your side, but I can tell you one thing. I will never treat anyone as if I own them. Maybe I am not that strong man you need in your life, Christina!"

"Let's take the trip first and see if we can determine who you are. Then Tony, we will see if you are who I need and if we can run this empire together."

"Okay, Christina, but you must know that if I stay, it is not for your money or your empire. It will be for you, and you will have to make some changes in the way you act and treat people. Do you think you can make that kind of change, Christina?"

"Tony, for you I can do anything, and I will do whatever it takes to keep you with me."

Emilio arrived just after Alva and Enrique left, he had been listening to most of the conversation between Tony and Christina from the kitchen balcony above them. He did not hear of Christina's plan to ditch Alva and Enrique. Once more, Tony has proven to Emilio that he is the man his daughter needs in her life and he feels more than ever that he has made the right decision in letting her go with Tony to California.

The next afternoon, they arrive at the dock. As they wait their turn to board the ship and begin their journey to Miami, Tony is taken by how beautiful and sleek the *Emerald Princess* is.

"Well, Tony, do you like the way she looks?" Christina asks.

"Yes, she is not only beautiful but modern too."

They pass the captain and his first mate, who are greeting the passengers as they board.

"Welcome aboard, Miss Milan. I hope my crew and I meet all expectations for you and your entire party."

"I am sure, you will do as great a job as you usually do, Captain."

"I see the captain seems to know you well," Tony says.

"Yes, before my dad purchased the *Christina M*, I always took this ship when I went to see my mom in Miami."

As they walk to their cabins, she grabs Tony by the hand. "You're not still mad at me over what happened yesterday, are you?"

"No."

"Good, I don't want them, or anyone else, to come between you and me."

They are scheduled to set sail that night for Miami. As they walk to their cabins, Christina grabs Tony by the hand again. "I want this to be a very special trip. One of many we will be taking together."

"I hope we do get to take many trips together in the future, and maybe in our next trip we can share our cabin," Tony replies.

"We can share the cabin *this* time—the only thing keeping you from me is you, Tony."

"No, Christina, I gave your dad my word. I may not remember who I am, but I know I am a man of my word, if nothing else."

"As you wish. Alva and I will unpack, and we can meet back in the lounge. We can go over where we will start our search once we get to California"

"Sounds good to me. I'll see you in an hour."

"Enrique, bring my bags to my cabin," Christina says.

"Yes, Senorita."

When Enrique arrives at her cabin, Christina says, "You and Tony will have lots of time to talk on this cruise. "

"Yes, I guess we will." He can sense she has something on her mind.

"You just keep in mind that if you tell him anything—and I do mean anything at all—you will be very, very sorry."

"Yes. I already know that, Senorita."

"Good, then, we have an agreement?"

"Yes we do," as he turns to leave her room.

"I am sure your grandmother will be very happy to hear that."

He stops and turns to see her with a smile on her face. "Why would my grandmother be glad to hear that?"

"Oh, I did not tell you?"

"Tell me what?"

"I spoke to the director of the adult community your grandmother has been trying to get into for the last two years. He assured me that, as a favor to me and my dad, she will be in at the end of next month. Of course, that is provided everything goes as planned for me and Tony on this trip. Do we understand each other, Enrique?"

"Yes, Senorita, I understand you loud and clear."

He puts the last of her bags inside and, and looks at Alva as he leaves, she out of her own fears just looks away. He walks out without saying another word. When he gets back to his cabin, he finds Tony there sitting on the bed and looking at the picture of the boys from the orphanage.

"Tony, do you think you are from California?"

"I don't know. At this point I think anything is possible."

"Tony, have you ever wondered if you are from Florida?"

"No, Enrique, is there something you know that I should know?"

He pauses for a minute and thinks of his ailing grandmother.

"No, it's just that we are going there first, and I thought you might have some memory of there."

"I don't know, Enrique. I guess we'll know more when we get there."

"Tony, may I ask one favor of you?"

"Why, yes, Enrique. If it's in my power, I will certainly do it for you. What's on your mind?"

"Well, sir, if we are able to find out where you came from, and that you do not want to stay with Senorita Christina, do you think I could possibly stay with you, wherever that is? At least, until I can find a job and go off on my own? I know people would talk, because I am gay, but I would not stay with you very long."

"Yes, Enrique. If I can find out who I am and where I am from, then whether I stay with Christina or not, you can certainly stay with me. I do not care what people may say or think of you staying with me. You saved my life, and that is the very least I can do for the man who saved my life."

"Thank you, sir, but if you do stay with her, then I will not need to stay."

"Enrique, I know she can be difficult at times, but all in all, you don't believe she's a bad person, do you?"

"All I will say on that is that you are a very good man, Tony. You deserve a woman who is as good as you."

There is a knock at the door.

"Yes?" Enrique says.

"It's me, Alva. Enrique, tell Tony that Senorita Christina is waiting for him in the lounge."

"Please tell her, for me, that I'll be up in five minutes," Tony says.

"Yes, I'll tell her."

After they set sail, Tony and Enrique arrive at the lounge to find Christina and Alva waiting for them.

"I thought the men were supposed to wait for the women, not vice versa?" Christina says to Tony.

"I am sorry. Enrique and I were talking, and I lost track of time."

Christina gives Enrique a stare, and his face goes white.

"Well, I know Enrique can tell lots of stories, some true, some not so true. Correct Enrique?"

"Yes, Senorita, but I was telling Tony about my childhood and how I grew up on the streets. How your father and my grandmother turned my life around."

"Yes, Enrique, thank God you had my father and your grandmother. How is your grandmother these days, Enrique?"

"She is fine, thank you."

"Well, that's enough of you and your wild life as a young man. Let's talk of the present and our plans to find out who Tony is and where he came from."

Just then the loudspeaker comes on and announces that dinner is being served in the main dinning area.

"I don't know about you people, but I am starved. Shall we go?" Christina says.

They make their way down the beautiful marble stairway that winds down from the third floor to the main dining room, which has a large crystal chandelier in the center. With people moving all around them, they make their way to their table. Once they sit down, the first mate walks over to their table.

"First Mate Antonio Lopez, at your service, Senorita Milan and company."

"Thank you," Christina says.

"Senorita, as a general rule we seat six people to a table. If it is alright with you, we would like to seat two more at your table."

"Do you have someone in mind, Mr. Lopez?"

"Yes, an older couple."

"Do you know where they are from, Mr. Lopez?"

"No, but I can find out for you before I sit them down with you."

"Please do that and get back to me."

"Why would you need to know where they are from before you let them sit at our table, Christina?" Tony asks.

"My father always told me it is good to know where your company is from before you sit down with them. This way you never sound silly or uneducated when you speak."

"Your father said this? That does not sound like the Emilio I know."

The first mate returns and says the couples are from South Dakota.

"You are right, Tony, this is silly," Christina says. To Lopez she says, "Yes, tell them it would be fine for them to sit with us."

As the couple makes their way toward the table, Tony notices a tall, slim, balding older man and his noticeably younger wife wearing a stunning low-cut red dress and pumps with four-inch heels, perhaps in an attempt to make up some of the difference in their heights.

"How do you do? I am Tom Taylor, and this is my wife, Helen."

Tony and Enrique stand up.

"This is Christina Milan, Alva Alvarez, and Enrique Fernandez. And I am Tony."

"I am sorry, Tony; I did not get your last name."

Tony smiles. "Well, that is a long story."

Tom replies, "Well, we have all night."

They all laugh. They sit down to dinner, and Tony tells his story.

By ten-thirty, all but a few of the guests have left the dining area. Alva and Enrique have excused themselves and retired for the night.

"Well, son, I have to tell you this was certainly an interesting evening, and, in all my years, I have never heard such an interesting story," Tom says to Tony. "If you ever regain your memory, you should write it down. I am certain it would make an interesting book. Don't you agree, Helen?"

"Yes, I do, and you are such a charming young man. I hope it all has a happy ending for you," Helen says.

"It will, if I have anything to do with it," Christina says.

Helen adds, "You two make such a lovely couple. I hope you both find the happiness you deserve, as a couple or individually."

"Well, Helen, as interesting as it has been, we must call it a night," Tom says. "I am sure you two young people want to spend some time to yourselves."

He and Helen excuse themselves for the night.

"What a nice couple. I hope you and I get along that well when we get to their age, Tony. It is good to see people married for that long still have so much in common and get along so well."

Tony gets up and takes her hand to help her up. "Well, I guess I will call it a night, too." He kisses her gently on the lips.

"Last chance, Tony?" She says as he walks away. He turns and looks at her. "Just kidding, Mr. Man of His Word."

Christina heads back to her room. She opens her door and startles Alva, who had already fallen asleep.

"Everything alright senorita?"

"Go back to sleep Alva, and don't snore!"

Chapter Thirteen
The Reunion

Karl hangs up his cell phone and turns to Safire.

"Well, doll face, you ready to knock them dead today?"

"Yes, I am."

"Good, I want you to do your very best."

"Karl, there's one thing—I want Javy and Heather in the front row."

"Sure thing, doll."

"No, this time I want to see them when I walk out. And I told Javy he could bring Maxx too."

"I can't let him bring some mutt to my concert."

"I thought this was my concert. After all, I am the singer, right?"

"Safire, you know what I meant."

"Sometimes, I wonder what you do mean, Karl."

"Okay, the dog can come too. It's just that I hope the ocean and the dog are not too much for you and you lose it."

"I will not lose it, but I wish you would have let me sing something else."

"That's what the producers wanted you to sing, and we have to go with that."

"No, Karl, I spoke with Scharla Nelson, and she said the choices were up to you and me. So I know 'Breathe Again' is all your idea."

"Safire, you will thank me later for picking that song. It is one of your best, and we need you at your best for your fans here and national TV. Let's go now. I have a lot of preparations to make, and I need to see where they want you to come in from and where to leave at the end."

The stage is set for her performance. Karl is making last-minute arrangements with the camera crew. She will come in by boat he tells the crew.

"This will be more dramatic. I need at least one camera to film her from about two hundred yards out, until she gets to the pier, right about here."

Camera crew supervisor, "Got it, we'll put Camera three right there. This way, we can swing back to the ocean while she sings, and her audience can see it on the twenty-by-twenty screens on both sides of the stage."

"Great! That's exactly what I want."

A security person taps Karl on the shoulder.

"What do you want?"

"Sir, there is a man here with a dog. He said he has permission to bring the dog in."

"Bring him here."

A few minutes later, Javy enters. "What? You're going to send me and Maxx home?"

"No, I'm not, but you keep that damn mutt out of sight of the TV cameras. You can stay over here by the sea wall."

"Would you rather I just stay in the water with the dog for the entire concert, Karl?"

"If it were up to me, you and your dog would not be here at all."

"It's Eric's dog, and it's not up to you, is it?"

Karl walks away. "Just remember what I said and keep that mutt out of sight."

Just one mile offshore, a small boat comes along side the Emerald Princess and a man jump on board.

Alva, "Why is that boat coming along side she asks one of the ships officers?"

"That is the harbor pilot, by law he must take over the ship from the captain and bring her into the port."

Alva walk to the upper deck and looks out the open-air stadium now coming into sight, as she begins to hear the music drifting ever so softly their way.

She turns to a fellow passenger "Who is that singing?"

"I don't know."

Another passenger standing next to them. "That is Safire, this is her fist solo performance."

Alva drops her drink and runs to find Enrique.

The ship is now only five hundred meters offshore. The passengers and crew can hear the music coming from the speakers placed all around the open-air stadium. The captain makes an announcement through the loudspeakers.

"I would like thank you all on behalf of the crew and myself for joining us on the *Emerald Princess*. As an added bonus, we will be passing by the open-air concert where our own Miami-born and -raised, lovely and talented Safire, is performing live today. If you would like a better view of the concert, we will be showing her performance on our wide-screen TV in the recreation room."

Enrique can't believe what he is hearing. Neither he nor Christina had any knowledge of the concert, but he now knows he must do something to help Tony.

Tony and Enrique are preparing to disembark. When suddenly Barbie's voice is being heard through all the loudspeakers on the ship. As Tony opens the door of his cabin and steps outside he can hear her singing their song, "Breathe Again," he drops his clothes and runs down the hall. Enrique runs after him with a big smile on his face.

"Tony whats wrong," he yells as he runs after him?

"I know that voice!"

"Tony, you do know her? I know you do. I saw a picture of you and her."

Tony stops and looks back at him and then turns and keeps on running. Enrique catches up and runs behind him.

Tony runs into a crew member in the hall.

"Quick were the TV recreation rooms?"

"Down this hall and to your left sir"

Tony runs into the now full room and shoves his way to the front with Enrique close behind him.

The camera is focusing on the crowd and then turns to Barbie. When Tony sees her face on the screen and hears her singing their favorite song, he turns to Enrique.

"That's Barbie!"

"Yes, Tony, that was her name before she took the stage name, Safire."

As Tony runs back out to the deck, Enrique pulls him aside. "What are you going to do, Tony?"

"I don't know, Enrique, but I know one thing I am not Tony. My name is Eric, and that is my Barbie on that screen singing."

Christina, upon having heard the news of the concert, is now frantically looking for Tony. She runs into him as the ship is passing by the stage. She holds his arm.

"My Tony, what are you doing?"

"I am not yours, and my name is not Tony, and I belong to someone else."

"No! Let's talk about this, Tony."

"I told you, I'm not Tony, and I belong to her, and I'm going to join her right now."

"Are you crazy? You can't jump off this ship. You'll be killed!"

"Watch me!"

He is now shouting Barbie's name at the top of his lungs and running to the stern of the ship.

On land, the music and Barbie's voice drown out Eric's shouts, at least to the human ear. But Maxx, who is at the water's edge, lying at Javy's feet, hears him and focuses on the ship, searching for the source of the yelling.

Christina shouts, "Stop him, he is going to jump overboard!"

A crew member goes to stop him, but Eric knocks him off balance and runs past him. A second crew member comes running from behind, but before he reaches Eric, Enrique trips him. Eric jumps onto the railing and shouts out Barbie's name one last time before he dives into the green sea below. He hits the water and begins to swim for shore.

Maxx, spotted him on the railing just before he jumped in, now, sees him in the water. He lunges forward and breaking free from Javy. He runs to the edge of the pier and jumps in without any hesitation and begins to swim out and greet his Eric. Javy, not knowing what has happened, runs to the edge of the pier and screams out Maxx's name. He looks past the dog and can't believe his eyes.

"Heather, come quick! Look, there is someone in the water with Max"

"You don't think, can it be, O my God it is, its him Heather, its Eric!"

The ship, not being able to stop in the middle of the channel, proceeds to deploy a lifeboat and crew members to rescue Eric. The ship's mighty air horns are now going off, and the *man overboard* alert is sounding off.

Karl hears the commotion and begins to swear. "Those idiots, what are they doing? They are ruining my concert!"

He runs down from the stage and past the security personal."What the hell is going on out there?" He asks one of the policemen on duty by the waters edge.

"There is a man and a dog in the water, look you can see them right there, I think the man jumped off the ship!"

"Jumped off the ship, what the hell kind of a fool would do that he asks the policeman?"

"I don't know sir, but I am sure we will soon find out, he and the dog are swimming this way."

"That damn dog, I told her this was a bad idea." He tells himself.

The cameraman who covered Barbie's arrival by sea now sees the drama unfolding in the water. He turns the camera to the man and the dog in the water. He focuses in on Eric's face, which is displayed on the twenty-by-twenty screen behind Barbie. The fans become excited at the ongoing drama unfolding before their very eyes. Some run to the water's edge to see the man and dog swimming toward them. Barbie, hearing the ship's air horns, turns just in time to see Eric's face as it comes on the screen. At first she is not sure of what she is seeing, then it hits her, it's him, he's back. She drops the microphone and runs to the edge of the pier where Javy is standing and yelling at Eric, "Come on, buddy! Come on!"

Javy turns and looks at Barbie. "What? Have you forgotten how to swim?"

"No, no I haven't."

She jumps into the water and begins to make her way to Eric. As they meet and their lips come together once more, Maxx swims around them, barking with joy.

Karl runs up to Javy. "What the hell is going on here? Is that Eric?"

"Yep! And I guess you're out, bud!"

"We'll see about that. And as for you … you couldn't hold that damn mutt?"

"Yes, I suppose I could have, but I didn't. Just like I could have held back from doing this!"

He pulls back and hits Karl hard with a right hook. Karl hits the deck of the pier quickly. "What the hell was that for?"

"That's for calling Maxx a mutt and for what you did to me and Heather in Atlanta."

As the sound engineer keeps the background music going, Eric, Barbie, and Maxx are picked up by the ship's lifeboat and brought to land as the crowd of shouting and cheering fans goes wild in the background.

The following week, Barbie reschedules her concert and gives the performance of her life, with both Eric and Maxx in the front row alongside Javy and Heather.

As for Enrique, he has a new job as Safire's personal assistant, and with Emilio's help has moved his grandmother to the retirement community. After a long phone call with Emilio, Eric has the pleasure of telling Alva she will be on a two-week paid vacation

to California to see her niece and her new born child. Christina has made plans to stay with her mom for a while to give her dad time to cools down after hearing of how she treated Alva and Enrique. And her ploy to make Eire think he came from California.

Chapter Fourteen
Home Again

As for Barbie, Heather, Javy, and Eric, now that they are all reunited doing the things they love most , they decide to spend a weekend at the four-thousand-acre West T"S ranch that their good friend Keith manages.

As they pull the horse trailer off the sandy road and onto a muddy buggy trail, Maxx, who is riding on a platform on the front of the truck, lets out a bark and leaps off. He takes off running through the palmettos and across the small slough into a water-soaked pasture. Water sprays up from behind him with every powerful stride he takes.

Eric hits the brakes, and the truck skids to a stop. As they jump out, and opens the horse trailer's doors and pulls the horses out. Keith throws down his beer and jumps onto the truck bed and turns Dixie and Minnie loose. As the two dogs run toward a palmetto thicket to catch up with Maxx, Eric and Javy jump on their horses and take off after the dogs, with mud and water flying in all directions. They aim their horses toward the stand of tall palmettos ahead of them, on the other side of the lush green pasture.

Eric ducks under a cypress tree. A limb hits his hat, which goes flying off. He turns his head and looks back to see his hat land in the water. As Javy catches up, he yells out, "There goes the hat. If you go next, at least this time I know where to find you!"

The End